CW00538467

BELOVED

EMPAR MOLINER
BELOVED

Translated from Catalan by
Laura McGloughlin

3TimesRebel

First published by 3TimesRebel Press in 2024, our third year of existence.

Title: *Beloved* by Empar Moliner

Original title: *Benvolguda*
Copyright © Empar Moliner, 2022
c/o Columna Edicions, llibres i comunicació, S.A.U.

Originally published by Columna Edicions, llibres i comunicació, S.A.U.

Translation from Catalan: Copyright © Laura McGloughlin, 2024

Design and layout: Enric Jardí

Illustrations: Anna Pont Armengol

Editing and proof reading: Bibiana Mas

Maria-Mercè Marçal's poem *Deriva*:
© heiresses of Maria-Mercè Marçal

Translation of Maria-Mercè Marçal's poem *Deriva*:
© Dr Sam Abrams

Illustrator photograph: © Comas-Pont arquitectes

The translation of this book is supported by Institut Ramon Llull.

LLLL institut
ramon llull

Printed and bound by CMP Digital Print Solutions,
Poole, Dorset, England
Paperback ISBN: 978-1-7391287-5-3
eBook ISBN: 978-1-7391287-6-0 / 978-1-7391287-7-7

www.3timesrebel.com

A CIP catalogue record for this book is available from the British Library.

Àlex, Gin.

Around Clarissa there were several people involved
in the serious events of the time. She, however,
had her son, so the small events were
what mattered most to her.

Clarissa, STEFAN ZWEIG

The morning sun when it's in your face
really shows your age.

'Maggie May', ROD STEWART

In the past he had ideals and emotions, and today
he has only a meticulous worship of hygiene.

Les bonhomies, JOSEP CARNER

SITTING IN THE MIDDLE OF THE BACKSEAT OF THE CAR THAT brimmed with signs of family routine (a well-thumbed, yellowing, electronics store catalogue, a folding umbrella on the floor, supermarket bags wedged into the seat back pocket in case our daughter vomits ...) I realise, one specific moment this afternoon, that my adored young husband will fall in love with the girl now sitting beside him in my seat. He doesn't yet know he'll fall in love with her. The girl doesn't know either. Only me. I know. I know he'll fall in love with her as he fell in love with me, and I haven't the faintest doubt. A rain as foul as fishmonger water is falling.

I think I've got to prepare myself for that moment which is yet to come but won't be too long in arriving, and I'm as certain as if I'd done a kind of marital pregnancy test. Rage? No, none at all, and even though I'd welcome it, rage is no longer a part of me. Upheaval, yes. Not resignation either, because even resignation seems too active an attitude. It's looking at things calmly, as if I were not the same person who fifteen years back was sick with jealousy for him. But I'm not the same. I've just remembered, because I swear I hadn't thought any more about it, I have the official card-carrying menopause now. And that changes everything.

'It's not considered to be menopause until a year has passed since the last period,' the doctor told me when, like all women, I'd gone and told her, like all women (we take feminine conventions very seriously), that my cycle was 'playing up a bit'. To him, my adored husband, I'd said nothing about it at all. It didn't need to be shouted from the rooftops. Given that he was ten years younger than me, I seemed to be usurping a decade of everyday life and menstrual contempt to which he was still entitled. (To 'usurp' is to take illegally or by force, I just looked it up in the dictionary). The doctor said: 'Come back when it's been a year since your last period.' And my period hasn't come in any of the months since, not even to say goodbye. But, fuck it, I was the same as ever, and I didn't go back. I didn't say it wasn't coming any more. I stopped saying it was coming.

Let's be clear. Until this moment I've been considered a well-hydrated, charming mature woman (yes, yes, I don't look my age, none of us do, everyone says so, we 'wear our years well'). I run sixty kilometres a week, go to Body Pump on Mondays and LBT (short for Legs, Bums & Tums) and take collagen pills, despite the studies suggesting their questionable effectiveness. I must point out that I find modesty overrated: I'm still a good deal. What's more, until now I've performed pre-feminist sexual positions with total dedication and delight. During bedroom fantasies I've revelled in being a prostitute, being used as a sexual object; I've said 'Possess me' in all seriousness, with all the sincerity of my heart and cunt, and done so with pleasure. All truly intellectual women (which we no doubt are) take for granted that we're good company and what we really want is a good fuck. More than anything I've wanted to be desired, and I have been. I already know I can be loved. Anything can be loved.

There's so much talk about the 'culture of hard work' and those my age will know this 'culture' well from now on, because we spend the whole day working hard. We've all been pretty in our own way; most of us still are. Everyone sees us as so limber that they don't realise there's a toe already bent by arthritis inside our trainers, inside our socks. Bye bye sandals! Hello podiatrist! Sixty-somethings laugh at us; they find we exaggerate to win praise, in the same way we laugh at forty-somethings (we find they exaggerate to win praise), but seventy-somethings laugh at sixty-somethings (they find they exaggerate to win praise). That's how it goes, ten by ten, until the end.

Not seeming old from now on, not appearing to be 'giving up' (it's a precise expression: it's you that lets yourself go), requires obligatory, blurry complicity from other women: younger, older, fatter, thinner women. Feet, hands, faces, double chins, heads. All these parts need the secret. Here is the definition of the 'mature woman': we can't pluck our eyebrows without glasses, because we can no longer see them up close, so to see the hairs we have to put on the near-sighted glasses. But if we put on the near-sighted glasses to see the hairs we can't see without glasses, we can't pluck them, because they're covered by the glasses.

Things as they are, my man is the first to remark on my apparent youth, and he does so with pride (everyone says we look the same age). Fifty-something? Not on your life. With this messy hair all hairdressers (the greatest and almost only sources of praise we have) rave about, athletic legs, a few delicate wrinkles, these eyes with no bags underneath (or not many if I haven't been drinking), posture careless as a jet of water, and this laugh, which is everything. Because we act with youthful nonchalance and a playful, infantilised attitude, nowadays no one our age appears our age. Partly a sign of the times, partly through medical advances.

I go out running and as I run I recall:

Death knells would ring, and eagerly, cryptically, nervously, our grandmother would say: 'Run, children, go and find out who's died!' The savage triumph of the survivor in her gaze. A tone of voice, more air than sound. She wanted to grieve, but she'd enjoy the moment before doing so. Someone had died and it wasn't her. My brother and I would set off to the church at top speed. 'Quick, children, tell me who's died!'

The gynaecologist must have been older than me — but I'm incapable of working out anyone's age — and she was thin. I say this because, while she was writing out blood test requests, she'd pause to advise me to do things she herself certainly did and especially those she didn't. Watch your diet, because 'eating the same amount as before' would make me gain weight now. And to walk ('try to walk', she said) for half an hour every day. That made me (who'd run twelve kilometres in the mountains that morning) purse my lips in arrogance and boredom. Who was she talking about?

When she pronounced her sentence, she warned me about what would happen if I didn't do the assigned tasks (namely, moderate my alcohol intake, laser off the hairs on my chin before they turn white, blood tests …), and I made a mental sketch: disobedient menopausal women — not me, naturally — turned into a kind of gnome. Shrunken and withered (due to bone decalcification). Hunchbacked and spiky (due to irregular fat distribution), with a lost gaze (due to myopia) and hairy faces but bald heads (due to hormonal changes).

'Request the following tests for Remei Duran: Blood count and composition, ESR, Prothrombin time, Blood sugar, Serum iron, Ferritin, AST, ALT, GGT, FA. Cholesterol, total and fractional.'

I completely forgot about it. I must still have the piece of paper in my wallet. It wasn't me. Everything the doctor said couldn't happen to me, or else I'd have to don a pointy hat and go work underground as a blacksmith.

And so this evening I'm waiting for my love at the place we always meet to go home together. We live in an ugly town on the outskirts of Barcelona, in the middle of a set of small, narrow, detached houses, part of a development that was never finished. Four houses, including ours, were sold. There are four more (the last one has squatters) lacking what are called 'finishing touches', because the developer stopped making payments and disappeared. We were the last to take the bait. There's a playground nearby in the nothingness, which was used to falsely mislead the buyers. We have a crusty communal pool that often turns green, because it's maintained by a very cheap company (we're only four contributing households, the squatters don't count) that only comes from time to time. The block of houses can be seen from the motorway, like a spaceship freshly landed on uneven ground. Its name is 'Swan Lake Village' and the vision couldn't be more tragicomic. Middle-class or hippy, who knows — it's a mediocre dream.

While running, I think:

Last year our daughter wanted a Furby for Christmas. She liked the idea of having a living being, the younger sibling who would never come, someone to show things to. The Furby was a pink and blue doll that used up a lot of batteries because it talked. It had many personalities. When it was changing personality it would say: 'Boo-tay!' It used to sing in Furby language: 'Eee-day, ee, ee, ee.'

We always meet in that square when we go to Barcelona to run errands. In the centre there's an ugly church, round and slightly elevated. A church like a roundabout, surrounded by cars coming and going. I usually sit on the steps to wait, but today it's raining so badly that I don't want to wait there. I go into a bar (an important detail), one of the kind wives like — wives who are not me, because I'm not a wife — to kill time. A bar with an orange juicer but no slot machine.

'A cortado,' I say.

I repeat the important detail: I would have been sitting on the steps.

And now the waiter naturally, routinely, innocently asks me a question no waiter had ever, ever asked me before:

'With soy milk?'

With soy milk. Fatal blasts of trumpets and timpanis echo in my head. I'm not used to ordering a Cortado, I always order an Old-fashioned, and in the places where they know how to make that cocktail, no bartender ever asks me if I want the lump of sugar they soak in Angostura before adding the soda water and bourbon to be brown, because they already know that if you're there, you're not worried about dying of a silent artery-related disease any time soon.

I imagined that one day, far in the future, someone younger would give me their seat on the train. And farsighted as I am, I'd already made the joke (the scrap of banal, exaggerated and satisfied banter that belongs to those of us over thirty) decades ago about the first time someone had called me 'lady' instead of 'girl'. Something like: 'Today a kid called me lady!' And you go on living and laughing.

But ... soy milk? Soy milk? I still wear jeans from before I was pregnant at thirty-nine, I have a skirt from when I was thirty, but the waiter has read some sign on my forehead associated with women in ads for pension plans: 'lactose intolerance', ergo 'menopause'.

With soy milk? I say yes. With soy milk. What can I say? I taste it for the first time, and it has a fake vanilla aftertaste that I unfortunately find extraordinary, excellent and, oh, dark and rough and strong jungle, I must say it: soy milk seems less heavy than real milk. There must be studies confirming that women like me, with 'my profile', contribute to the prosperity of the industry of this misnamed soy milk in its pink-coloured packaging, dreamed up for the whole army of furious, eccentric gnomes with requests for blood tests lying forgotten in their wallets. Now I have scientific confirmation of the volatile state in which I've found myself for the last year but not paid any attention to. Falling oestrogen, combined with lactose intolerance and loss of near sight, makes me see the world through the light wings of a dragonfly. Because of this I can see, with utter clarity, that my man is going to fall in love with this other woman.

My brother Felip called me a liar, I think to myself as I run. He said: 'You like the attention, you want the universe to revolve around you, liar, bitch.' He doesn't want to talk to me. If he comes across my comic strip in the newspaper where I work as a cartoonist he tosses the page away.

My young husband has double-parked in front of the Nespresso shop which has such polite, over-friendly workers, whom I see toiling away from the stone bench of this ugly church. Sometimes we make fun of the shop workers, he and I. We speculate on the chirpy reaction they would have to an armed robbery. The horn sounds beep, beep, while the attractive lady I still am, this time on a bar stool with the soy milk Cortado already drunk (as foreseen), pays no heed to the fact that it's our car. I don't recognise it, I'm light years away from knowing its registration and make, all I know is that it's white. I feel flattened (perfect expression), but nothing is threatening me yet. I take it for granted that my failure to recognise the car will be as hilarious, as familiar, as ours, as it always has been. Me playing the spontaneous one, the direct, vibrant woman, all that, and him playing the perplexed lover, the one shaking his head, smiling, because no, no, he can't believe that *she* is like that. But this time it is different. No music video.

She's a violinist. The girl sitting in my place (who he will fall in love with) is his new desk-partner at the orchestra where he's had a permanent post for the last ten years. She's the stand-in violinist (a friend of the conductor's friend's daughter, it seems) who is coming home to rehearse. Danger indeed. All female musicians are sexy. All men have drooled one time or another over imaginary double bass players (always barefoot) playing pieces with sweet vigour.

They sit in pairs when a concert is performed. One music stand for every two musicians. It so happens that the desk-partner who's sat with him until now has lung cancer. My man is happy about having a substitute. He doesn't like his partner at all; he says he stinks, doesn't study, is very neurotic. He wishes him dead, half in jest.

I leave the bar and smile at everyone and no one, because I've still not detected the new passenger on our ship. Two metres' distance from my eyes is all fog and unknown land; likewise the span of two hands. I can't see far without glasses, but when I put them on to see far, I can't see close up. So I wear contact

lenses to see things a little less clearly at a distance than I
need to, because then I can see a little up close. The result is
that I see neither far nor near very well; I can only make out
things the width of a hand away. In general, the world I see
is much uglier than it really is. A white gull on the sea looks
like a plastic bag to me; our dog cringing in a corner, my
black sports bag; a red toadstool, a BabyBel wrapper; poplar
leaves on the ground when I run on winter roads, red starfish
someone has thrown away; those of the plane trees, brown
and straight-stemmed, dead rats; the creative, thick, square
jewelled necklaces some women wear, passes for congresses
or trade fairs. My brain has become unwillingly accustomed
to premature, perverse interpretations.

He told me this morning the girl was coming to our home
to rehearse and make fingerings on the score (they note
whether the arc goes up or down, so they go in time) but I'd
already forgotten. How am I going to remember a violinist
if I don't remember more pressing things like where I left
the keys to the door of my cave?

He's happy to rehearse with her, have someone to take the
work seriously with, because he's always complaining about
orchestra life, sitting in the last row of second violins. He says
it's like being in an army: no soul is required to play (but on
the contrary, I find they all play very soulfully). Senyor Hilari,
his stinky sick desk-partner, never wants to do fingerings.
I'm happy too, because I want to see him excited (a decade
younger than me, he also feels like he's getting old, not the
same way as to me, before me, at a more dangerous age than
me: forty-something). Anyway, I always like musicians coming

to our home. If there's music I'm happy. I like music much more than him and I'm an illustrator. But he likes comics much more than me and he's a musician.

I walk quickly towards the car, the way women in heels do (we manage to go slower when running than when walking). I smack my forehead with the flat of my hand — a sweeping, hyperrealistic, clichéd gesture to demonstrate that I'm scatterbrained in a nice way, mocking myself in front of the new spectator. 'Now Mama's going to get into the wrong car,' our daughter used to predict when she was smaller and they were waiting for me. Because (I say it now I don't have my own oestrogen) I've made them laugh a lot. Living with me has been marvellous, a riot, that I can say. But today is different. Today it's as if that message that comes up on websites warning you about the cookie policy has found me in the middle of the sky. It asks you: 'Close and accept?' If you want to continue surfing you have to say 'Yes'. You close and accept. And my story could end here.

I open the back car door making over-the-top squeaks and grunts like a quivering dog, to demonstrate my happiness at being sheltered.

'Didn't you see me?' he says.

And it's a didn't-you-see-me full of reproach but also outrage and a little exasperation. He's never said that before, or perhaps I've never noticed before now. I'm still focusing on menopausal onomatopoeia.

'Nooo!' I cry, pulling out a cliché of happiness. It's a *no* meaning: 'No, of course not, you know what I'm like, I'm ... Oh, what am I like!'

The violinist moves as if to get out to give me the spousal seat. I refuse with my customary grace.

'Not at all! I'll go in the second violin row. Today you're the concertino.'

She laughs very freely. I've made an in-joke (the concertino is the soloist). Less forthcoming, he purses his lips and with the flat of his hand he smoothes back his long hair with the same gesture as always. It's completely useless because it instantly falls back where it was. Then he runs his hand over his beard, which is as long as a beggar's. When I saw him for the first time, I thought of him as Neptune from the Trevi Fountain (I say it to him every time I see him in underpants or wrapped in a towel). He's so like him I can't help imagining the statue's hair and beard of white marble as parquet-coloured, like his. And like that tranquil God, he has immense feet, an immense head, immense hands and arms; he is a super-sized God (his genitals aren't visible). As the statue is standing, we don't know what he'd be like if he bent down, but I want to think he'd be like the triton beneath driving a winged horse and blowing a conch to make way for him: stooped, with a little loose belly fat. His belly is like that, and I'll always like it. A little paunch, like a half-deflated ring abandoned in the swimming pool over winter.

The sex I've had with him has been what I'd have with a marine god. Someone large but nimble and careful, calm until provoked, grunting and slow. He's so like Neptune that for a laugh one birthday, the little one and I arranged to meet him on Carrer Neptú, a street named Neptune, and if they have a 'Neptune pizza' in a pizzeria we always want to order it. I draw a trident and crown on him in photos we take at the beach. Their benevolent, morose expressions are also similar, although that god is doing a task like pacifying the waters that you imagine to be tense. For Neptune, calming the waves seems as routine as handling the steering wheel is for him now. I don't know how to drive at all.

Not yet. I've not yet seen what must happen. With complete levity and faith, the soy milk is coursing through my veins. I breathe in a vague feeling of danger in the atmosphere, as if someone had sprayed this danger into the air. Particles of danger are already falling, already raining down on me. I perceive them as if they're soaking me, because they have this insecticide smell, but I still don't detect it. I smell him, pheromones I suppose. Danger has always made me cough and sneeze.

I take off my coat, make myself comfortable in the car, fasten the seatbelt and so on. I'm about to see it.

While running, I think:

The first night we went to bed together, once we'd finished the first encounter (first day, lots of encounters; first few months, lots of encounters; first few years, lots of encounters; last few years, few encounters, one encounter a week, one a month, one every three months) he touched my back as if he were a butcher. He said: 'This is the loin, good meat would come from here; it should be cut here and here.' And with his hand, like kids playing shopkeepers, he pretended to be cutting. 'This is the liver, we'd make it into pâté. Good thighs, lean meat would come from here.'

None of the men who have gone to bed with me, at all the different stages of my life, have managed to move me like he, my young husband, did that first day, but of all the men I've slept with, he's the only one I was already in love with on the first day.

I learned that there's nothing in life like making porn while in love. Nothing. To explain it, I think of the music he plays so routinely that I like so much: it's like hearing Beethoven's *Missa Solemnis,* especially if you believe in God. My love says there's a moment in this mass (we've listened to it in bed a thousand times) where 'Beethoven makes a harmony that's already Wagner.' And he always repeats, laughing, laughing, one of the few times he laughs: 'Here Beethoven steps out of the century.'

I stick my head between the two seats, his and hers. I pinch myself, I touch my ears to be certain they haven't turned pointy, because I can't believe it.

'Will you make us a wee cocktail when we get home?'

I'm asking because the 'Didn't you see me?' has alarmed me. But why did I have to use that diminutive, why?

He says nothing. He often leaves me as 'Seen' on phone messages and in life, too.

'Well?' I insist. More silence. 'Òscar?'

It's a friendly way of letting the violinist know she's welcome, I'm happy she's coming, but also warning her that this is how we are, he and I: we make cocktails when we get home. That we're a duo and with the little one, a trio; we're like those shrink-wrapped packs containing foods that go well together, like a punnet of strawberries and cream in a spray can.

'I don't know. Do you want one?' he says.

Such a rational tone my love has today.

'Do you like cocktails, Cristina?' Me, insistent.

Her name is Cristina. What a pretty name. How nice it sounds. Not too classic, not too modern. Cris. Cristina.

'Ooof! I get drunk in no time,' she answers.

Him agreeing with her:

'Ofcoursecoursecoursecourse. Maybe better to rehearse first.' Turning to me: 'But if you want I'll make you one. Will you want one?'

Only a few days ago, we'd have been united in sarcasm if she said 'I get drunk in no time'. Yet 'another woman' who doesn't drink. Who wants a San Francisco, who doesn't know any of the cocktails we like. A forever joke in our home: 'How can my husband play a concert while drunk?' I ask. 'Because I always rehearse while drunk!' he answers. We've wholly despised those who weren't like us two until now. Few women drink with as much awareness and wisdom as me, and this trait has always made me more of a man's woman. This, football, dirty jokes and the fact that most women have always considered me a potential danger (and considered me so for all the former reasons). But just now he said 'Ofcoursecoursecoursecourse.' He doesn't want one. He doesn't want one? Suddenly he's like Cristina and not like me?

While running, I think:

How many men have I gone to bed with? I can't remember them all and it doesn't depend on what they meant to me, but on the order in which they came. I don't know if it's because of the menopause (all loss, it seems: of calcium, of love, of eyesight, of memory and who knows what else), or because nobody remembers all their sexual partners if they've had more than, say, ten.

My first husband — a decade with him —, my second — maybe another decade, I don't quite remember. With how many did I cheat on the second? How many were there before the first (whom I left for the second)? Doesn't everyone say that you always remember your first love? Who was the first lover in my second marriage? I don't remember unless I actively 'think back'. I don't remember who opened the tap that suddenly made me a probability for all the others that came along and for whom, unlike the first, it was so natural that I would be unfaithful.

Is it not more relevant to recall the first lover than the first love? Anyway, all of them — every one — have been something else, something different, and nothing to do with Neptune who is, no doubt about it, my last love.

But I remain fixated on the cocktail because perhaps I already realise this woman isn't like others.

'We'll make it weak,' I tell her. So annoying, so drunken (so old?). 'How do you like them?'

'I don't know much about them ...' And she smiles a young, tense, patronising smile.

Another phrase that would have made us covertly, playfully,

pinch one another's arms. I look at him through the rearview mirror but he doesn't look at me. He strives not to, he doesn't want us to gang up on her. Not on her.

'What kind of alcohol do you like?' I ask anyway. It's an instructive interrogation of those who don't know cocktails like we do.

'I'm very odd. I like bitter things.'

And suddenly his face lights up:

'Like Remei!'

Like me (mine is such an ugly name, *remedy*). And he looks at her with eyes I know well. The eyes from that first night, when he was the butcher. Like me. Like his attractive wife who likes bitter things, but never would have dared — even if she wanted to flirt — to say 'I'm very odd.' It was considered a beautiful idiosyncrasy of mine from first knowing each other, the bitter thing, because he's all about sweetness. He'd invent cocktails for me, with Campari, Cynar or grapefruit. He'd give them names in English containing the word remedy, a remedy for his Remei.

That's when I see it. I see that she (with pink-tinted hair like a groupie from the 80s, and tattoos on her neck and arms that would be vulgar on any of us but look sublime on a violinist) will make him lose his head. He will fall in love with her.

Everything will end. All my sophistication suddenly disappears. What does it matter what I think, what I feel, what I like, how I behave? The political problems surrounding me that I draw in the newspaper comic strip and discuss with my friends when we go running, where are they? I become simplicity itself. Flat. From now, I'm just waiting for what must happen: my man will fall in love with the girl sitting in my seat. No big deal.

I look at her. She's a new, young version (more predictable, with easier and more intuitive functions) of what I used to be (not physically), of the artistic part he liked about me that's still there, but in another way. A new phone for the same SIM, where everything is better optimised, where you have to re-enter all your contacts, transfer your photos. You have this entertaining work to do.

He'll want to take her to bed and he'll look at her liver to make it into pâté, too. Or maybe foie-gras, with her. Different to his wife, to me, and also because over the years he's become more thrifty, in theory. This is going to happen, and he still doesn't know it. But why will it happen? Because, since she looks like me, he won't feel so much of a cheat? Or because, as he likes a certain type of female artist, he accidentally always falls in love with the same version of the song? He still hasn't noticed — but he will when they start rehearsing — that she's left-handed, like me. That was a prized rarity at the beginning of our marriage (because I draw with my left hand, of course). Everyone likes us lefties.

From the backseat I look at him. Since I have no plan as yet for the terrible immediate future, I merely think that if he does as he did when he fell in love with me and left his girlfriend, this Cristina will soon suffer on my account. For I did suffer a lot because of his ex. He'd call to comfort her on her loss (which was him) and do domestic favours for her (that he's never done since at 'home') like putting together IKEA furniture in her new single girl's flat, I imagine with adorable ineptitude. Thinking of her helplessly laughing despite everything, because, for example, he said there were too many leftover screws, killed me. When they used to weep on the telephone (she because she'd lost him and he because, egotistical as he is, he understood her pain), there was a stream of ritual between them that excluded me. What did he call her? Love? Honey? Baby? Little one? Simply, Anna? What?

She'd call him at four in the morning and tell him she couldn't sleep. He would get up, make himself a cocktail (then, yes) and tell her he was rehearsing a piece by Mozart. She'd answer (I could hear her because of course she'd wake me up too) that Mozart seemed too predictable to her because 'she could see him coming'. I, who knew nothing of his musical day to day, envied them in the same way I'd envy the Curies, whom I imagined invariably alternating conversations about shopping lists and about polonium.

He left her for me, but he swore — and I believed him — they were like two cousins who loved but no longer desired one another. (Could that be said of us two, now?)

I had all my oestrogen then; therefore fury, constrained fury, rage, fear. I had to crush her, that ex, but crush her in a way that didn't hurt, because pain is productive, so that couldn't be, she had to crush herself, be wounded and afterwards be fine. On the contrary, today with Cristina I'm no more than the still, dirty dog's water in the bucket. Then, completely jealous, with no fissure for a rest, to relieve the pressure; jealous, jealous, full of rage and evil, chock-full of hate at all times, clutching my belly so it wouldn't burst and spill my entrails all over the ground. I didn't want him to speak to her, I didn't want him to recommend sleeping pills, not even an overdose of sleeping pills (I couldn't bear the absent presence if she were to die, or the idealising or photos which of necessity would remain in the secret compartments of his wallet and the sleeve of his violin case); I didn't want him to have more of a past than the one we two didn't yet have; I didn't want them to have ever gone to a campsite, as he casually told me once; I didn't want to hear the word campsite; I didn't want them to say 'that campsite'; I wanted campsites not to exist, but I also wanted them to exist so I could hate them, so they could be destroyed with fire and bombs. I didn't want to find dedications in books or I'd have to tear out the pages and then tear out my eyes. I wanted me and him to have rituals, history. I didn't want to hear any opinion on Mozart, because he'd known Mozart with her; Mozart should never have existed.

She represented domesticity; I the artistic life. She drank too much, me not much (but now, like her, I'll soon drink more than him). Fifteen years later, I'm beginning to flicker, I'm about to go out: I'll shift to domesticity (two artists cannot live together with children, without one ceasing to be so). Cristina will be the artistic life. It's only a matter of time before they go to bed together, she starts drinking and I, finally insomniac, see Mozart coming.

So, sitting there in the back, I start to calculate how I need to prepare myself, but for what? A dirty war? Trying to prevent it? Resign myself? Forgive it? Leave him? Kick him out? Kill them? Pretend I didn't see it? Suggest some previously forbidden sexual favour? Let him sodomise me regularly? Do it doggy-style, but with a mirror on the ceiling? I'm already a gnome: every option seems great, every one painful.

Her. Yes, let's talk about her. Not yet thirty, I'd say. She's physically the complete opposite of me. She's plump, and it's already clear she always will be. She'll be a plump old lady. One of those women who say they're 'curvy'. I'm a fraudulent thin woman. With a fake normal complexion. Truly with all I eat and drink, if I didn't do so much sport I'd be some kind of crab (disproportionately long and thick limbs stuck to a small round body). Not her. Having cleavage and haunches really suits her … Her. So innocent, so infuriating, so self-assured, so eager to please, so sweetly soft. She has precisely the grace of never having done any sport (and she's definitely one of those who say with pride that running 'is for cowards'). She's like a bride or a sheep being fattened up for a wedding or the oven. She wears thick black plastic glasses, which make her eyes as naive as my little girl's Furby. Without the glasses, she's like a nineteenth century peasant. I mean that in a good way. She's one of those women with such a Catalan face that it makes you imagine her acting in the classic play *Terra Baixa* by Àngel Guimerà, with a basket of corncobs on her hip. Let me correct myself. It's not that she resembles a nineteenth century peasant. It's that she resembles an actress playing a nineteenth century peasant. Round red cheeks, large breasts, very fine hair (that's why it's dyed). The 'natural' look.

I can't say anything bad about her, except that maybe the timbre of her voice is a little too sharp. She's not communicative, she's docile and loving like a baby mammal, but she has evil eyes; she'll show no mercy if she feels attacked. We don't know what she'd be like without me in the way. Whenever I meet someone, I try to determine if they ever cry and from what. If my man cries, it's from pain. The little one from frustration. She cries from rage (I cry about everything now). She's not intelligent in the same way I am. I have the partial intelligence of a hustler; she has the partial intelligence of a mathematician. He likes intelligent women, or more to the point, he'd never like a woman who wasn't intelligent. That will make everything easier. If Cristina were less intelligent, I'd be more belligerent.

But before going home to make the bitter cocktail (which we'll both grasp in our left hand), we have to go pick up our daughter from school. Cristina already knows and doesn't mind. We stop at the toll booth.

'Can you get the card out?' my young husband asks.

The card thing has also always been the source of a joke between us until now. I never remember I'm the anointed one in charge of taking out the card to pay the toll on the way home.

I give him a card.

'No, no. Not that one! You never remember, do you? The La Caixa one!'

Head spinning, I look for the La Caixa one, worrying I've lost it, or won't find it, because he'll take it from me in front of — I say it — the other woman.

I find it. I give it to him with the same ceremony and pride as if he were a drug baron and we were getting ready to cut a line of cocaine newly arrived in port. He tuts, but not because of me, no, I've not done anything; there's a driver in front of us who doesn't know how to insert the card in the slot, and this makes him impatient. He can't wait even ten seconds to rehearse with Cristina.

'How can she not know how to do it?' he cries, completely perplexed.

Inwardly I smile: because the woman is a gnome like me. She obviously can't see up close. She can't see where the arrow is on the card that shows you how to insert it. It must be left to chance, I know the feeling. That arm going out the window is menopausal, at a more advanced stage of decay than mine. The crepey skin I'm guessing she has makes me think she's definitely swapped spinning for aqua gym. But what about me? How long do I have?

On the train I observe old people and youths (now I say youths?) to see how they behave when they need to get off. Old people get up one stop before theirs, start putting on their coats, some take out their keys. On the other hand, young people brimming with oestrogen and androgen, get up at the last second; they pick up their jackets (which they don't put on), inadvertently bumping into the arthritic, brittle knees of the passengers opposite. The owners of the arthritic, brittle knees (jackets neatly folded on laps, about to be donned and fastened) moan, so hurt. The young people carelessly apologise, but the owners of the knees don't forgive them, they'll never be able to forgive them, and they'll continue moaning in the carriage, while those on the platform will have already forgotten them for ever more.

Merciless, my young husband gives me back the card without turning. He doesn't want to show her anything of what we are (nor what we have been or we would be) except errands and coldness.

He double-parks at the school gate. I can see the fastest kids already coming out, full of energy, straying, waiting to be collected. It's dizzying to imagine all of them as grown-ups. This boy, that girl, all adults with strange hardships like me, like Cristina. Mine is always one of the last to come out, slowly. Every child behaves as they behaved during labour. If they had to be pulled out with forceps like mine, they'll make you tie their shoelaces, never be in a hurry to leave class, always waiting for a hand on their neck to push them: 'Go ...'

'Don't take long, *please*? I'm badly parked,' he tells me. And by saying 'please' in English in front of Cristina he ceases to be my love, Neptune. He's someone I don't recognise. Someone who says please in English. And anyone saying please in English no longer has the ungainly testicles and penis they've always had; he doesn't have them if he says please in English, if he says please in English his dick is stashed away, always predictable, dormant in his underwear until someone orders it to stick its little head out.

But right then it doesn't matter because I open the car door and on putting my foot on the ground, the fairy casts her spell, little sky blue stars make a loop around my head, a harp plays to emphasise the magic and the transformation occurs: now I'm a mama. Nothing else. A mama. It happens to us all with very few exceptions. I still have the 'First Class Mamas' chat from when she was six on my phone; now in the final year of junior school, we're still the same. A category everyone jokes about: all men and also all women (those who don't yet have children, those who won't have them, those who haven't had them, those who had them a long time ago, those who wanted to have them, the Cristinas who haven't even thought about it yet, and ourselves). Before having the little one, I joked about them too. Mamas. So annoying, so obsessive. Indifferent to the desire we provoke. If we paint our lips it's to go to the escape room for Maria and Guiomar's joint birthday. We gossip, we compliment outfits, haircuts, the ability to make cakes or organisational skills, and we spur each other on in starting diets or never doing so, in introducing quinoa to our table; we criticise Magalí's mother who lets her daughter be a YouTuber; we know the names of the other kids in class, and we ask each other, with the necessary dose of irony and desperation, for photos of the pages of homework our kids haven't written down in their journals. We wish each other a great day with absolute sincerity. I like dissolving into this group, not sticking out like an unblended lump. Being the most distinctive, I'm the one who likes it best, the one who is most likely to feel up to taking some rice to the food bank.

At first, I went to the children's birthday parties feeling indifferent and unwilling, but not for long: later on I was happy to meet up with everyone, drink beer from a cooler on the grass in parks where we host the girls' informal birthday parties, and chat — what an incomprehensible pleasure for the rest of the world — for such a long, long, long while about our children. We didn't foresee parenting becoming our drug. We *want* to parent. Normal, working, bright women who have lost their heads about their children. Women who've had them later than normal (some have had to undergo painful, expensive, difficult procedures to do so) in a dangerously mindful way. With an overwhelming awareness of doing an activity as intellectual as it was instinctive. We don't want to share the badge of motherhood, we don't want to find a balance, we don't want positions of responsibility, we never want to be separated from the litter; we secretly cried the first day of school, we would be housewives if we could allow ourselves. We need puppies that come to us so we can remove lice or fleas, and we prefer removing lice and fleas to commanding the world. This is feminism's main stumbling block. It has to count on these lionesses, junkies for parenting like us.

'It's like when you taste the lobster in *caldereta*,' I explained to our running mate one day. He has a daughter, but he doesn't want to be with her every minute like us; he often gets tired of her and palms her off on his ex.

'Why?' said he, who moves through the world not comprehending its mysteries and mechanisms, and is untroubled by his lack of understanding.

'Because *caldereta* is a sailor's stew; sailors used to make it on board, using what they had while they fished. Nobody wanted lobsters, but objectively they were good. And now this humble sailor's stew is a high-end dish in high-end restaurants, since everyone values lobsters because they're very expensive. And due to the context anyone who tastes it feels something different to that sailor, because they're also doing it intellectually. This is what happens to us being "mothers". It's always been like this, but we're hyper-aware of it.'

'I've never had *caldereta*. Is it good?' he said. He eats only rice and chicken, to gain muscle. He's a personal trainer.

Some of us will stop seeing each other when our daughters go to secondary school next year, because at secondary school there are no longer mothers at the gate. What will we do? Walk the surrounding streets like zombies? We've been this way for almost a decade, which has passed in a flash. Being fifty is nothing. Being sixty, sixty-five is nothing. What is everything, what is vertiginous and irreversible is the litter being fifteen, eighteen, twenty. That indeed is like coming off drugs. Then, when there are no more lice and fleas, only bad words that must and will come, now alone with our partners, if we still have them, we'll go to cultural events, feed cats and drink cups and more cups of soy milk, always held in both hands to warm us up.

Gretchen, one of these mothers, is there. Once we've dropped off the kids at nine we go out running almost every morning, and we've become better friends through running than if we'd met in a bar, where we probably wouldn't have liked each other. It was she who persuaded me to try it. And now I realise (I'd never thought about it) that she hasn't had a period for years because she had cancer and they had to remove her right breast and ovaries. She's German, but she came to Barcelona seeking sun for her freckles, not knowing anything about Catalonia, thinking we took *siestas* and danced *flamenco*. She landed in this town of ours where she opened a macrobiotic shop. She learned Catalan (with a grammar book for children I'd just illustrated), devoted herself to eating *calçotades* of barbecued onions and tomato-rubbed bread, and she gave Catalan names to her two little daughters. Two names almost every Catalan gives their children and which she struggles to pronounce: Montserrat and Núria. 'Mountsi, Mountsi! Núrria, Núrria!' she shouts.

At first we were shy about running together in case we didn't have anything to say to each other. It seems unbelievable now, because we never shut up while running. Then Dani, the personal trainer who'd never tasted *caldereta* (also a father in our class) joined us. More than misfortune, blood, work, or political struggles, sport brings people together. All the women and the odd man that he trains fall in love with Dani — he's so sweet while correcting postures, so close and intimate when he touches a muscle so you feel it — and he's happily gone to bed with them all (he can't help but find women who do sport and wear expensive clothing appealing). He and Gretchen would never have made friends. She would have found him very rude and a climate-denier, and he'd have thought her too square and too passionate about recycling. In contrast, Dani and his type (Dani has confessed that when he goes to bed with a woman, he checks out his own quads in the mirror) make me laugh. But at the end of the day they love each other, accept each other's jokes, help each other, sometimes drive each other mad.

When we'd been running every morning, summer and winter (whether with lips numb from cold and hands limp or with faces smeared with sunscreen and a water canister on our belts) for a year, a new girl arrived in class. One of her two mothers, Francina, was very sporty (as is usually the case in couples, the other wasn't at all). One morning we saw her dressed in sportswear when she was dropping off her daughter and we invited her for a run 'to show her the tracks around town'. Although she's a reserved woman whose reserve makes her seem shy, she always comes when not on the night shift. She's a firefighter.

Our daughters — Mountsi, my Angèlica, Carla, who is Dani's daughter, and now Francina's Aarushi — aren't friends, they only tolerate each other. We've tried and it didn't work. Aarushi was a novelty for a day or two, but now, if any of us say anything about the backpack (Aarushi carries 'such a heavy' backpack) and how she likes to cook and how responsible she is, the other girls get jealous (they all want to be the centre of attention) and say it's not such a big deal.

Until now, if something extraordinary happens and the four of us don't go out running (if I have an illustration to submit, or they have an order of quinoa to receive, some fire to put out or some lady to slim down), we send each other messages with tiny bits of news: 'I've eaten like a pig', 'The teacher says the little one hasn't done a thing this term', 'Mine wants to sleep with us', 'I have a new client who wants to invite me for dinner at a Japanese place'.

Gretchen instantly asks me what's going on. Dani isn't there, because on Mondays his daughter does an after-school Cookery in English class and he comes to pick her up an hour later (Francina is late). Anyway, Dani wouldn't have picked up on any change in me. He's one of those people who doesn't know how to express condolences without laughing, or hug, or be there at sad times. His wife left him because of his infidelity and because when his daughter was born, he wasn't coming home before 2 a.m., overwhelmed and incapable. But he trained us and stayed with us all the way through our first marathon to the finish line (we crossed it holding hands), even though he could have gone much faster. The laughs and newly minted slang afterwards were priceless. How we laughed, sitting on the steps of the Torres Venecianes, dead from sore feet, wearing our ponchos and medals.

'I'll tell you another time,' I tell Gretchen (because I-can't-deal-with-please-in-English, he's double-parked with his future love). But will I tell her?

'Tomorrow?' she asks me.

'Tomorrow!'

Every time we go running we mostly talk about her life and her relationship with one of the squatters in the squat on my street. (Her husband hasn't slept with her since the cancer). The squatters living there have a vegetable patch with an old-fashioned scarecrow in a hat (but nowadays no bird is scared of a doll in a hat; birds have lost their naivety too), and they walk badly trained dogs in the park where she brings her, by contrast, very obedient dog. That's where they met. He's an Italian boy who goes topless in long skirts almost all year round. Our adored friend makes him wholemeal cakes, hummus (she has a knack and a persistent, incomprehensible affinity for making hummus) and brings him 5-litre drums of water, because they have none. On her way home after spending the night there, she takes the rubbish and throws it in each corresponding container. At parent dinners she's very taken with her husband, who is blond and handsome like a Viking. One of those men who love children so much that at the park he lines them up and puts them on his shoulders so they can reach the net and score a basket. Mine would never do that. He's never wiped a snot that wasn't his own.

I greet the little one, who comes towards me (deliberately) slowly. Everything else disappears when she appears. I ask her a bland question: 'How was your day?' My mother never did that with me. How was your day? And how should it have gone? She didn't come pick me up; nor did she let me sleep in her bed, as I still do with mine, on any pretext (more and more often her father sleeps on the sofa), no doubt to save me the realisation that now I'd need truckloads of oral oestrogen to feel like oral sex.

'Great.'

She always answers that way. Then, me:

'What did you have for lunch?'

Her, already bad-tempered:

'Aw, Mama, always asking in front of everyone! I don't remember!'

'Then think! It's not like I want to give you a Michelin star is it, sweetheart? Just that if you had chicken for lunch, we won't have it for dinner.'

Saying this. Being able to say this. Until when?

While running I think:

I demand over-the-top love because I had a ruinous childhood, and I say ruin in the sense that someone says, for example, 'you've ruined a painting or a dress'. Now because of that, now I appear to be a mature woman, my ideal storyline is the first ten minutes of a film, before the catastrophe. The prelude. The picture of happy rituals that exists only as a necessary precondition to disaster. The woman speaks to her mother on the phone as she makes a cake in the beautiful, overdone kitchen. The son plays basketball.

Hours and hours like this, with no plot twist, not a single one, with no kidnapping or hit and run ever coming, seeing them eternally live a normal life.

Yes, yes, the double-parked car. We move towards it ('Quick, quick, Papa is in a hurry!') and from afar I can already hear one of the pieces they need to practise playing. They always play three: one contemporary, written by some composer friend of the conductor, which I always find unbearable, and two good classical ones. Shostakovich's Festive Overture (ta, ta-ta-TA, ta-ta-TA ...) is playing. It's very cinematic, for dramatic moments when waters part, when traffic lights turn green as you approach. Sometimes when the little one does things well I tell her it's playing in the background like a soundtrack (I can still say things like that to her; I won't be able to as soon as she gets her period). I know it's one of the three pieces they'll be playing, because I've seen the email with the score printed out on the kitchen table. Until now, I've always looked at myself from above, as pleased as an omniscient narrator, never quite used to scores on the kitchen table. I've loved him being a musician.

We get into the car. He says hello to the little one — hello for *her* — but before starting the car, he makes an observation about the violin part to the girl, to Cristina.

'See how he must be *faking* here?' And laughs.

She smiles incredulously. She'd not thought about the possibility of faking; she assumed study and more study was required in order to play so many notes in a row, but now he, the experienced sly dog, the cheating musician, tells her the trick. Faking! Deceive the conductor so he doesn't see that you've not played all the notes (no one plays them all, he assures her).

He's showing off in front of me. He's showing me he's an artist (but I've never forgotten ...). He's still an artist if she is, and then I don't fit in.

'Above all, don't look him in the eye or he'll never believe you!' he roars.

How they laugh. I realise it's been a long time since I saw him in a laughing mood. And so I realise my days are numbered. Even slipping on a banana skin I'd no longer make him laugh.

In our house, the third on the unpaved alley (named after a Balkan republic), we have a basement that the architect certainly thought would be used as a cellar, but he's converted into his soundproofed studio. Cheap houses, because they're well outside Barcelona and not very near the train station, for people who buy cheese and wine and bath salts on offer at the supermarket. Therefore small cellars and small bathtubs. Promises of the good life, full of 'personal' moments, of scheduled pleasures that, after the ardent novelty, always end up being too much effort. He records melodies and rehearses in there. There's a small sofa (where they'll be able to make love, uncomfortably) and busts of composers, bought in the Encants flea market, as a joke. A papier-mâché one of Beethoven I made him. They hurry down there. There'll be no bitter cocktail.

'What do you want as a snack?' I ask the little one. It's so strange to me that they're both down there, making beautiful sounds.

'Something *healthy*,' she says in English.

She makes me laugh. She always speaks in English with humour in mind. I extravagantly celebrate her good humour, because it's starting to become rare.

'An apple?'

'No! Not THAT healthy ...!'

'Bread with tomato and susaaaage?' We say susaaaage not sausage.

'Cut very very thin, see-through?'

I uncork a bottle of cava I don't want to end up finishing off. Finish up finishing off. I have to be more moderate, I have to bear the Pythagorean cup, the greedy person's cup, in mind. I also put out a bowl of crisps, the glutamate addict (I do the same thing, I seal the bag with a clothes peg and stash it in a kitchen cupboard). When she hears me chomping in my study beside her bedroom, the little one comes to graze, like a mewling kitten. My wine glasses and my drawings are part of the domestic routine for her. We set to work: she to do her homework, me to illustrate a passage of Moby Dick for a textbook.

'My breast bud hurts,' she says after a while.

'That's normal,' I tell her, while I make a white whale's tail emerge from the black waters. 'Come on, concentrate.'

And her:

'Aw, Mama ...! Besides telling you ...!'

She's not surprised by how beautifully I paint the world. It must seem strange to her that other mothers don't.

No doubt the two of them, my man and the girl, the male and female violinists, Òscar and Cristina, Neptune and the nereid, are at work and nothing else, not holding hands, not looking at each other in a daze (they're looking in a daze at the score, with so many quavers they're obliged to fake it) because right now it's the work that's sensual: sharing it, finding solutions, getting annoyed, tutting at the difficulties. Passing each other the headphones. Beginning with that transfer. Everything is biology in disguise. Intelligent people first woo through culture then the body comes into play, because the physical attraction is actually already there. The cultural preamble is what changes everything in doing so simple an act with such limited variations as sexual coupling: a unique, radiant moment superior to eating, drinking or dying. Biology invents this 'pleasure' thing so you can't stay away. What a strange pleasure. We do everything for this pleasure? We live for this pleasure. And then what? It disappears and we scoff dessert at all-you-can-eat buffets.

In the orchestra, the musician on the left is the one that turns the pages of the score, so for that moment they stop playing. The one on the right, seemingly more important, doesn't. In the orchestra she'll sit on his left. Her stinky, dying predecessor Senyor Hilari used to sit on the right. He hated this, because he considered it unfair.

After a while I hear the basement door open. Neptune leaves his marine palace and rises to the surface seeking a glass with ice for the whisky he has below (a whisky I gave him, a special whisky) in an antique cabinet, and an iced tea for her. He pours it into a glass — he always peers at the crockery, a habit he's inherited from his mother — with a twist of lemon. I feel awkward garnishing glasses or plates. Like displaying cleavage, or even worse, feet.

'Ah, you've opened champagne?' He asks in the voice of a father.

'Yes, are you having whisky?' I answer in the voice of a maître de.

Two pieces of evidence. Two needless questions. No to a cocktail, because it's what links him to me. Yes to a whisky, because like me, he needs alcohol.

He also grabs two of the little one's Kit Kats and puts them on a tray, with a paper towel underneath. For her. I find this alarming. I never imagined him doing so religious an act as making her an offering of sweet things.

They have so much work they don't have dinner. And since he normally takes care of dinner, and it's a known, accepted and certified fact (until that day, happily so) that I don't know how to cook, have no ability and my contribution to family life is basically economic and psychological, the little one and I 'decide to sin' (we always say this): we order pizza. Such a happy pair in front of the gigantic computer in my studio, choosing (even though we always order the same thing) then her making the order, trying to sound adult. Unwillingly remembering that just before I'd briefly agonised about preparing a balanced dinner.

By 'psychological contribution' I mean that I used to contribute — I can no longer say it in the present — an acceptance and empowerment of other people's quirks. I accepted and empowered — because it made me happy — the way he was, the way the little one was, the way my in-laws were, the way his sister was. I like everyone, in one way or another. He likes hardly anyone, in one way or another.

Today, however, I finish the bottle. We both eat the pizza like gluttons, along with the dog, who snaffles up everything she can. It has parmesan sauce and strips of breaded chicken, and will give us a relentless, scorching thirst all night, and definitely, definitely, definitely wreak havoc on our bellies. We both make the same expert comment:

'Unbeatable.'

I find her saying such a grown-up word she's picked up from me funny.

'Yes, they're unbeatable.'

'Really unbeatable.'

'Unbeatable for sure.'

While running I think:

Four years ago, a mother in the park asked: 'Seriously, which do you prefer, orgasm or massage?' And everyone laughing at the irrefutability of the answer, said: 'Hell, massage!' I looked at them without participating. I wasn't like them. Not at all! How could they laugh about giving that up? Why did they condemn themselves like that? I felt closer to the husbands who'd have said 'Orgasm!' Or 'Massage and orgasm!'

That night when she and Neptune finish pacifying the waters and reappear, he tells me he's going to drop her at the station in the car (walking to the station at night is scary, it's a good fifteen minutes away on foot). He sees that I'm full, with that physical stupor after you've eaten badly and an attitude of not wanting anyone to see you've been drinking on a day when you shouldn't. He says nothing. Only his eyes, watery from the whisky, reproach me.

But he takes his time in coming back, so much so I realise he's ended up bringing her back to Barcelona. That's a relevant detail too. When his parents and my father come up for lunch at our deserted outpost, he never takes them to Barcelona. Too much faff to go to Barcelona and back; he drops them at the station. He must have brought her to the Gràcia neighbourhood, where it's so difficult to park. Where must he have left the car? In a car park? Maybe, maybe not. He'll search for a parking spot for three quarters of an hour with us. That's made me laugh until now. But now that he's gone to Gràcia to bring Cristina home and they've probably decided to 'have a bite' and he's found a carpark so as not to waste time, it's a future comparative grievance: I'm obliged to be exasperated from now on. No longer will him searching for a parking spot be funny when he doesn't do so with her. But I'm inhibited by the lack of oestrogen. Deep down I understand him. I understand I should call it a day. Close up shop, they say.

And once alone (the little one is already in bed and we've chatted, both under the covers as usual) I get a headache that I first think is a mix of hangover and fatalism then work out is a psychosomatic flu. All of a sudden I'm very very tired, very weak, and I notice my brain is fuzzy. I feel like floppy cotton, it's what everyone says and couldn't be more precise. I'm revolted by the pizza (the word *pizza* makes me gag and I can't get it out of my head); I've no strength, but definitely a fever. I'm never sick. I've not been sick once in the last six years. I know because for the last six years not two days have gone by without me going out running. I immediately send a message (contact lenses in, so not seeing up close) in the chat (with the photo of all four of us at the marathon finish line) I have with Gretchen, Dani and Francina. 'Giys, I'm sixk, O csn't cime runnng.' And Gretchen, who can't see up close either, writes: 'Tak cre if yoeswlf, thwn O moght go sponnng.' 'OK' from Dani. Francina hasn't seen it, or finds it over-anxious (and therefore unseemly) to answer straightaway. There is an encrypted menopausal idiolect only Dani understands, adept as he is in training women like us.

All of a sudden I start coughing a lot too. Of course you never realise the exact moment it appears, but I do because for the first time in my life with this very dry cough, I fully understand ads for incontinence pads.

This is it. It's been years since I coughed and I didn't know, it hadn't even occurred to me, what happens to a woman of my age (who runs and has given birth) when you cough this way. They told me about laughing, but not this. All of a sudden it's happening to me. All of a sudden. Not little by little, as it should have, to have time to get used to it and sign up for hypopressive gymnastics and buy a box of vaginal tablets. A quaver of trumpet and timpani. And those ads I've always found humiliating seem so friendly now. I'm the same person I was a day ago. Yesterday, in a jeans outlet shop (cheap because they're the ones worn by mannequins) I tried on a pair in size 8, because they were lovely and because I wanted to debut a pair when going to the hospital to see Senyor Hilari, the stinky, dying musician, but, above all, because they fit me, dammit. Or I fit into them. I fit into them! Adolescent brands, like a young girl (like an old woman thinking she's a young girl) emerging barefoot from the fitting room to look at myself in the shop mirror; everything suited me; everything suits someone size 8. But what if I don't see myself as I am in the mirror? I bought four pairs and I was very happy. I already have them, I can already stain them with the next bout of coughing.

Overwhelmed, I go to the toilet; the gurgling of the old bath pipes laugh at me, because even if I don't see it I'm old too. I don't know what to do first: put a wet towel around my head to bring down the fever, or throw the also wet leggings in the laundry basket (I go — used to go — around the house barefoot when I wear — used to wear — leggings, because I am — used to be — an attractive mature woman who doesn't — didn't — like any underwear lines visible on this saggy ass toned by body pump classes with a personal trainer and friend). Legs bare, I sit on the toilet, towel on my head like a turban. I suppose I look like a fakir.

The little one (I still call her 'little one' and I'll call her 'little one' in the care home, if I make it there) comes out of the den in search of milk (she never stops drinking milk) and finds me sitting there, legs akimbo.

'Have you taken off your pjs?' she asks me.

She says *pjs*. Drunk as I am, my eyes fill with tears. I anticipate the future sorrow when she stops saying this within a year or two, when, ashamed and furious, she figures out that her mother sometimes drinks too much.

And me:

'I'm coming down with something, I'm sweating a lot.'

I can't think about anything except that now everything is beginning to end (if I feel maudlin talking about these losses, I don't feel maudlin talking about the others); now, suddenly, from one day to the next, one hour to the next, right on time, no sooner or later, I've become old, and like the soy milk waiter, my man has sensed it, doesn't yet know it but has the urge, is obliged by nature, to spread his seed in other pastures, similarly cultivated pastures in this case, before it's lost forever. She sits on the rim of the bidet and sips from the glass. There are two bathrooms at home (one absurdly bigger than the kitchen) and this tiny one which is 'ours'. Immediately the dog, who cannot be more than two metres away from me, comes in. The vet told us that she has 'separation anxiety'. Me too.

'Poor, poor ma ...' she says. And she hands me toilet paper to wipe myself. 'Here.'

We've always had this faecal transparency. We comment on farts (categorised by sound) and shits (by texture), the sounds don't bother us and the stench makes us laugh joyously, scandalised. We can say the word *poo-pellets* quite naturally. That's how we used to be, before Cris (bC). When one sat on the toilet, the other waited alongside. He considered it very uncivilised, disgusting; he didn't want us to do it; he would get mock-angry if we did. I used to tell the little one the Romans had public, unisex toilets, with no separation in between. Strangers sitting side by side, chatting and sniffing one another, maybe. That would have been great for me and her. Two toilet bowls, one beside the other. And maybe we should copy them. He'd shout in horror — truly horrified — when he heard us and complain about the scatology permeating this Catalan land in which we live, in the children's stories I illustrate where children are eaten by bulls and expelled with farts, in the characters that shit beside the baby Jesus in the crib, in the folk songs about whether shit smells in the mountain. All those things that have existed since time immemorial and make Gretchen and the Viking laugh in sincere bewilderment. Now I find myself with this, and we haven't made any folk song about it or have any story to illustrate. We have:

> *A monkey way up*
> *With his bum rolled up ...*

We have:

> *A fart from the cow's bum*
> *And out came Tom Thumb.*

But we don't have, nor will we:

> *You wet yourself at fifty*
> *in a coughing fit or laughing*
> *despite with Kegels you've been grafting.*

I can tell her a few drops came out (and she'll tell me not to worry about it), but I can't tell her I was asked whether I wanted soy milk and also her father will fall in love with a fertile nereid with pink-tinted hair, who she'll find adorable too, more adorable than me. One day she said to me: 'Do you want to be my best friend?' I knew the mature response should have been: 'I can't be your best friend, because I'm your mother,' but immature as I am, I said yes and we bought rubber bracelets that said 'BFF'.

While running I think:

Stopped. This is how we say it. My periods have stopped. Because it gives a more precise idea of what's happened. They pull out, they disappear. They don't leave, don't exit the stage to applause. Do you miss them? You miss what you were; you miss complaining about them, despising them, being inconvenienced by them. One week having one and one week saying it's on the verge of coming. So for half the month you justify your bad mood and bad-tempered reactions if anyone asks if you have it. You make an announcement when they first come (maybe your mother does and you're embarrassed about it) but none when they depart. Periods. There was a — short — span of time at the beginning of your conjugal life (the conjugal life of the same person you are today) when they didn't even prevent sex.

I wipe myself, but start coughing again (a cough that begins in the diaphragm and causes pain in my muscles) and more streams out. I can't stop coughing. Cough, cough. Such friendly onomatopoeia, like in the comics I have around the house. I haven't coughed like this in years. A dog's cough, dry, constant, like a tic. When I finish the mechanical manoeuvre it's as if I haven't had quite enough and have a desire, a painful desire, to cough again; I can't avoid it, try to avoid it, a spasm rises within me and I don't want to, but how long can I go without doing it? If I hold in the spasm, I talk like a ventriloquist.

'Go on, go to bed, it's very late,' I say.

When I say this I sound exactly like my mother. I have her quiet tone of resignation, a tone that carries the weight of atavism, the unfairness of life, and having had to live with dirty, gaseous, merciless, surviving relatives at the muddy farm, from the first day of married life. A tone fatigued not by any physical scar, but by one of the spirit. I do it on purpose. It's a homage to her greasy memory, for the granddaughter she never knew — and I can't work out whether she would have loved her fiercely or considered her, as she did me, nothing more than a useful link in the chain — because she died very young of a 'malignancy' (that's what they used to call cancer).

The face I remember is a blurry still. A photo with me, her eldest child, on her lap, in the little house where we lived all crammed together, with that resigned, inexpressive smile, appropriate to the occasion. 'Childhood is the homeland,' writers always quote when they're interviewed. They say this in reference to the author, who was dressed as a girl until the age of five during said childhood. For him, the homeland was forced transvestism. For me, it's windows with broken glass covered with newspaper, rabbit urine and the shouts of my uncle, Tiet Ventura. She never drank alcohol, my mother, unlike my father who did; she never went out for dinner or entered a bar; she never wet her head under a shower; her hair was always done by a mobile hairdresser from the town, who used to come every fortnight with all her tools. She always stank of rarely washed clothes, rarely changed sheets, worn stockings, a brown tubular girdle and certainly something for incontinence too. She liked coffee and that was all. She used to say 'a wee coffee'; this was her luxury, the diminutive, a pretence of normality. I don't understand those who talk about the enigma of Mona Lisa's smile. It's exactly like my mother's. Mona Lisa smiles that way because she's a broken housewife. Broken housewives smile like that.

I put on a pad, but it's not absorbent enough; it's not prepared for this continuous cough. What will I do tomorrow? Will I be well enough to slip out to the pharmacy in secret? Because I can't tell my love to stop listening to the *Missa Solemnis* and do me this favour:

> *Kyrie eleison*
> *Christe eleison*
> *Ithi agoráze spárgana*

Which is more or less:

> *Lord, have mercy*
> *Christ, have mercy*
> *Go and buy me nappies.*

From bed I hear the car arrive. The Festive Overture at full blast. They should have their own raves, classical musicians. DJs spinning minuets and requiems for all kinds of patrons with perfect hearing.

'I-think-I-have-a-fever-I've-been-really-worried-about-you-I-didn't-know-where-you-were,' I tell him. Of course it's a lie. I wasn't worried; I knew where he was.

Nothing has happened, yet. But will he tell me when it does? It won't be necessary, I'll know. He can't deceive me. And besides, I know the feeling (from the accumulated experience of deceiving my second husband) when you fall in love with someone else. Of pretending you don't feel like it, even though it seems you'd never want to get caught, and even though, if you get caught or they tell you they suspect, you deny the evidence ('You're paranoid, you're jealous and no one can live with someone so paranoid and so jealous') because what you don't want, the only thing you don't want, are the scoldings, the reproaches, the pouts or the tears and promises. Deep in your heart you couldn't care less if you get caught. Actually, you want to get caught, because you have such confidence with the cuckolded husband (brother by now) that in your irreplaceable shared confidence you want to explain the marvellous thing happening to you that (sadly) affects him.

'In the end I brought her home and we had a hotdog.' And he adds: 'After all the work she did, poor thing ...'

The protagonist of the conversation isn't my sudden illness. It's the 'poor thing'. The hotdogs. I imagine it was fun. Intimate. That asthmatic wheeze of the pot of ketchup. The delicious simplicity. She asked for a *bikini* (ah, how it disgusts me now). Those ham and cheese bikinis are a first-date sandwich, because they're not difficult to bite with half-open mouths. Few women will let eating remove lipstick on the first date (I'm one of those few). Cristina must still be too embarrassed to bite and chew in front of him; no doubt later on she will. But maybe they said to each other: 'Do you want a taste of it?' If she was the first to say it, the phrase might have been: 'Do you want a taste?' No 'it'.

And he certainly accepted and she didn't. A small, prudent, modest bite. If it were me, his wife, letting him taste her sandwich, he'd have taken a bigger, less prudent bite, in no way modest (the confident marital bite of the sandwich, trying not to take the whole slice of ham, always trying not to, of course).

I could have let slip a jealous-spouse 'Uh-huh' but I don't. This is the first decision I take, without thinking. Not to be jealous. But I'm really not.

From his breath I know he's drunk beer ('we' had always found it easy to drink beer). What had they listened to in the car? Bartok, maybe. He likes him a lot (because he's difficult) and I don't at all (because he's difficult). It could be my Mozart. It could be Cristina's vengeance and security. New spouses spend their lives opposing their predecessors. This is the unsung, bittersweet triumph of exes. Snoring used to annoy the predecessor, and now you can't be annoyed, it's-that-she-was-a-bitch. The predecessor wanted to paint the kitchen blue. You want that kitchen white, you hate blue, can you believe it. The predecessor saw Mozart coming, you consider him humanity's greatest genius.

Hugging him right now, putting my hand on his ass will be considered a reaction to what has happened (what hasn't happened but is already there), and he'll think I don't feel as bad as I'm saying. I do it anyway. I touch his ass, because that ass is mine; I've licked it, licked inside the folds because he

likes it, I know and no one else in the world knows he likes
that, and now maybe in time she'll come to know it too. I curl
up on top of his torso and he's immediately erect (although
he probably finds me suspicious). This is the true wonder of
him. Instantaneous reaction. As far as I know, many men
have unsolvable problems with their mothers, or their exes,
or their baldness or stature or bellies, which are directly
reflected in their penises. Not him. He's a natural. We've
already said he has a very fat body. His musician's suit looks
adorably dishevelled on him (Neptune would have to get his
jackets made to measure, they couldn't be bought from a
department store on the seabed as he's done). He throws it
together the best he can and looks like a beggar. I suppose
this is also one of the reasons he's made to sit in the last row
of the thirty-two violins (two rows of eight music-stands)
with Senyor Hilari. If they were in the first row, the women in
the audience would be searching for a cap to throw coins in.

One day, the guest conductor of the orchestra, an old
gentleman and lover of Catalan folk dance, looked at them and
cried: 'They look like two *vagabonds* ...' The word *vagabonds*
made me cry with laughter, it was so precise and so out of
place. I was in tears and couldn't even speak. My sides hurt
from laughing. How I could laugh like that, then. He'd said
it in such a strong Catalan accent ... bC, sometimes the little
one and I, as a joke, just to be annoying, would stand in front
of him (moving in sync) and say together: 'They look like two
vagabonds ...!' then run away.

As I touch him, I think when Cristina falls in love with
him (she'll fall in love with him on discovering that he's in
love with her) she won't fall in love with this, the deflating

tyre that is his belly; she's not intelligent enough. I also think he'll try to hide it. He's not intelligent enough. He'll want to slim down. How sad.

But surprisingly, the sex hurts. The last time, two weeks ago (or maybe three?) it didn't hurt. The gynaecologist asked me that day and I told her: 'No, no!' Now, today, all of a sudden it does? Everything is happening very fast. Tomorrow on the computer I'll see banner ads for funeral plans.

'Am I hurting you?'

And I have to say yes.

'Yes ...'

Yes, I have to say yes. It hurts too much to pretend it's nothing or disguise it as pleasure.

'But what is it?' he asks, very apprehensive. He doesn't want to hurt me. He would never want to hurt me.

'Don't worry, it's an age thing,' I say. I feel dizzy, paralysed.

We end with fellatio. As background music, the piano section — which is, well, more Arabic — of the Festive Overture plays in my head. I could say I try to make an effort, but I always make an effort. I like doing it, because he really likes it (but what man doesn't?). I like seeing him unable to bear it. I suppose all ladies end up being good fellatrices, or not at all, and of this the repeated, secular experience of older women comprises: we're categorised as 'hot matures' in porn.

'You need lubricants when you're pre-menopausal, that's all.'

I said 'pre'.

'Anyway, it's common knowledge that women's libido decreases around then ...' he murmurs, very understanding.

'Not in my case,' I lie.

'Look at my mother ... I bet it's been fifteen years since she had sex and she's very happy.'

His mother is nearly seventy. I'm in my fifties. But now he puts us in the same box.

His mother. Her name is Aurèlia and I find her very forward. She's a singing teacher, and the exact illustration I'd do of a 'fastidious' lady. She always goes to museums on her own, and tells me about the things she's seen (she values my drawings more than anyone else in the world). She's very conceited, one of those women who adore canapés and cava, who have a trusted butcher from whom they buy 'shavings' of ham, and the same hairdresser for years, who is the only one who 'understands' their hair (black and frizzy like a pagoda). When she travels she says: 'We've done Prague', not 'We've visited Prague'. There is always a box of lozenges on the piano for her students. At first she thought that — as an artist — I'd think of her son as a fling and soon get tired of him. Now she loves me and knows it'll be the little one and I who wash her if some day she can't manage by herself. Her children and husband won't do it.

'What about your father?' I say.

'We men are different,' he quickly answers. 'I'm sure my father has his resources ...'

A bout of coughing comes over me and I hurry to the bathroom.

While running I think:

Energy cannot be created or destroyed, only transformed, and orgasms are energy. What do orgasms transform into when you no longer have them? Those every-night orgasms that used to help you sleep well and you no longer need. Prune roses and tidy if you're of a certain bent or carp and take offence if you're of another? I don't see myself pruning or tidying, or criticising and being offended. I suppose all I can do is draw and drink, not forgetting the Pythagorean cup in either case. It's a cup I bought in Athens airport, when I went to a conference of female illustrators one time.

The following morning, weak and slow, I rummage through the bathroom cabinet and find an open packet of sanitary pads, way in the back. I'd not thrown them out, of course. I'd find another in my case or in my backpack, in my gym bag. I suppose there comes a time when the yellow-coloured wrapping (we've all ended up buying from the same sanitary pad monopoly) grows even yellower and you throw them away. Maybe cleaning someday, after years have passed. Or maybe you keep them just in case for your daughter, if you have one. It's unnatural that by the time she gets her period you no longer do, but that's how modern society is now in our corner of the world. So it's been with me. I've done everything a good ten years earlier or later than due. Now she'll be an adolescent with mood swings because of her period. I'll be menopausal with mood swings because of the menopause. Smothered, he'll crash into Cristina's arms. Cristina seems a lot less crazy than us two, though.

While running I remember:

'I've put up with it for a long time, now it's your turn to put up with it,' my mother told me. I was eight. She was referring to her brother-in-law, my father's brother, Tiet Ventura, who lived with us and wasn't all there (what a lovely expression). It was always said he'd gone crazy during the war, when Granollers was bombed. He was a child when he and a female cousin were caught in an explosion in the middle of the street (his older cousin died instantly).

This is what she said: 'Now it's your turn to put up with it.' Her tone was resigned, tired, as if she'd said: 'Now you have to get to work.'

Put up with it. I knew what she meant, because I'd seen her do it. She didn't hide it, maybe thinking of that replacement, too. She and my grandmother used a phrase, a euphemism, when they were referring to 'putting up with it' (which is exactly what it was). They'd say 'fixing him'. 'Tiet must be fixed'. 'Must be'. Not 'I must'. Sometimes: 'Oh, Tiet must be fixed.' Like an extra farm chore (and it truly was an extra farm chore). I didn't know the word, the sexual aspect, defining what I'd have to do to him now. I discovered it years later, when I was already living in a child protection unit, looking up dirty words in the dictionary.

Harlot: Prostitute.

Prostitute: A woman who sells her body.

Now, dictionaries (all online, of course) have adapted to the times by including a masculine definition. What Dani does from time to time. Not that I know all the details, but he says there's a certain pleasure in knowing he's being paid.

Screw: act of twisting or turning to tighten something.

(Disappointing, that one).

And that word. When I read it — it's accurate — I fainted. That was fixing my uncle. I fell to the floor and when I came around I had a bump on my forehead and all the carers were asking me if I was OK. And I was coughing. I couldn't stop coughing.

My mother used to do it, then it was me who used to do it, because he couldn't, with those chicken hands. Fixing him. If I protested (I used to protest), if I whimpered (I used to whimper) or if I hid (I used to hide) when it was time to do it — always after school (definitely after snacking) — she'd routinely come find me shouting, espadrille in hand, as if I'd done something naughty, with none of the attitude someone knowing they were asking something depraved might have. When she found me, she'd say in that tired voice: 'Oh, come oooooooonnn ...!' And if someone buying eggs or milk, maybe knowing nothing about it, asked why I was being scolded, she'd shout wearily as if she had nothing to hide: 'She knows why!'

Tiet would be very happy when he saw me. He'd be shrieking in the chair where we always kept him, like some kind of pet (and I thought of him as such). Given the chance, I preferred fixing Tiet than fixing (really fixing: cleaning) the rabbits, who used to have a stench of piss that would make me, disgusted by nothing at all, vomit even now. Given the chance, I preferred fixing Tiet to helping to kill them, those stinky rabbits, because it meant grabbing them by their ears while my grandmother hit them on the head with the mortar, and waiting, anticipating, to see how she'd make a slit on their legs and skin them, as if she were pulling off pyjamas (pjs). I preferred fixing Tiet to changing his nappies which we nicknamed the 'package' (the worst on the whole farm), to cleaning the chicken coop, to helping during the pig-slaughtering, with those scratches the poor fattened beast would bestow before being tied to the table where its throat was to be cut, which made me think it already understood and was anticipating its destiny. I preferred fixing Tiet to lots of things, but I used to make up homework to avoid fixing him. That was the secret to my excellent marks, and it proved useful because my first husband, who more or less rescued me from the streets, paid for my university degree in Fine Arts: as if there are any Ordinary ones.

I learned the procedure straightaway. First with my mother's hand guiding mine (a mother's wise teachings are never forgotten). Later on, all alone. She always criticised my lack of strength — even with the skill for drawing everyone acknowledged, I still didn't know how to peel an apple properly, with my thumb on the flesh, or tie my shoelaces, and I'd already learned to fix uncles — so I always did it with both hands. If I complained that it was disgusting, or my hands were tired, my mother would give me a slap (an out of context slap, a slap terrible in its normality, a firm but routine slap, like when you rob chocolate, for example, a somewhat friendly slap) and say to me:

'So little skill, girl. What'll you do when you get married?'

While running I sum up:

First two years with Neptune. Love and sex (always combined), music and alcohol.

Third year: Pregnancy. We give up everything, decide to change our lives, and we watch our first series at night under the covers, like everyone's been doing for a while.

Fourth year: she is born. We name her Angèlica, after Angelika Kauffman, the eighteenth-century painter who painted herself having to choose between music and painting. It was what we were imagining for her (everyone thinks their child is a genius).

Sixth to tenth: We live a charmed life of health, spontaneity and mystery. I become 'her mother' and nothing else.

Like this:

I went to school meetings and wrote down the bags that had to be brought in a notebook: one for a change of clothes (big, labelled); the lunch bag for fruit at snack-time (small and labelled) for socialising; one for the smock that stayed at school until Friday, when we took it home to be washed; one for white-soled sneakers for psychomotor learning (small, labelled).

We took her to paediatric check-ups; we bought games that developed her imagination, always a year ahead. I taught her vocabulary using a method of my own invention. When

she said: 'Ta', I said, 'Ah, you mean "star"! You said star!'
And I drew a star. And every time she babbled (ddd), I said:
'You said dog. You know how to say dog. This is a dog.' And I
drew a dog. All the words she said incorrectly would forever
be a part of us.

We would take her out in the buggy for a walk, completely
in love. Sometimes she slid down until the strap separating
her legs touched her nappy. She liked it, it gave her pleasure.
She would move. I didn't know whether to reprimand her or
let her do it. I was surprised that not everyone was looking at
the buggy; that they didn't step aside from our path, paying
us tribute, like the peasants I drew for the story of *Puss in
Boots,* when they see the Marquess of Carabàs' carriage go
by. We painted the walls of her room, she and I, with all kinds
of fish and a Neptune, of course. Then we'd shower together,
but we didn't mind being dirty. She wasn't yet disgusted by
my naked body, she didn't yet say I was a chimpanzee. I sang
her made-up songs, the most glorious of which went: 'You
do pee-pee, I do poo-poo', which shows I'm to blame for the
scatological case she developed as she got older. I asked her
father to tell me what notes they were. He told me. He played
them to me on the violin as if they were jazz. He recorded
them for me. He did everything I asked him to do, then.

We took her to concerts and comic conventions and she
would behave so well. We immediately gave her a small
violin to play, and those pencils that look like watercolours
when wet. What will she choose, what will she choose? When
we played *Clair de Lune* she smiled in recognition. We had
a children's book of famous paintings including Angelika
Kauffman's self-portrait. She is in the centre, and on one

side, Music (represented by a resigned woman in red who says with her eyes: 'You're making a mistake ...') and on the other Painting (represented by a woman in blue, with an expression of 'Let's not mess around! Let's go paint!') From the sadness on the painter's face, looking at Music, and how she's showing her the palette, with her hand open, (an open hand saying 'It is what it is') we understand (and know) that she's chosen painting, but with regret. If I showed her the painting, the little one babbled: 'Angelika Kauffmann!' and I'd applaud. It was like potty-training a dog, but I didn't realise that at the time.

She made that painting at my age, fifty-something, but she painted herself as a girl of fifteen. A madwoman like me.

As soon as I knew I was pregnant, we decided to change our lifestyle and move outside Barcelona, to a house where he could rehearse, far away from the bars and the dealers, far away from the sweet repetition of the highs and lows of artificial stimulation. How artificial everything that came from it was: the happiness, the anxiety, the absence of tiredness and boredom, the words, all of them, the mirrors in the toilets of the bars where you could see eyes as beautiful and bright as a mouse's, the toilet seats that everyone bent over to snort cocaine, the clothes that were worn expressly to be taken off at the end of the night, the omnipresent porn. We wanted 'security', we wanted to be middle-class, we wanted to live by day, worry about the world, emerge from introspection and sociability, the lullaby of the night. Go shopping by car once a week to 'stock' the fridge. Have a vegetable plot, more as an idea than a reality. We wanted to change together.

The director of the children's publisher I illustrated for, who was the author of two novels and a professor of literature, lived in a development in a town north of Barcelona with very cheap houses. There were still some available: why didn't we take a look at them? We took a look and were pleased. We liked the public school where he was still working then. We'd take the house and I could hand him illustrations through the window. It seemed amusing.

Neptune took the entrance exams for the orchestra, and got a permanent position. He also gave violin lessons to children and played accompaniments — engagements, they call them — for singers. I took on all the illustrations of all the textbooks I could. Romans and serfs for History; Jesus walking on water for Religion; Pythagoras, without his cup, thinking under a tree ... A job for a plastics company, too: I drew shower curtains, beach bags and individual table mats. Paper boats, butterflies, kiwis and bananas, smoking diners. Everything.

We had help from the in-laws. Expressions like these (down-payment, help from the in-laws) turned us into an ironic middle class. We thought the house was ugly, but in an amusing way, and it meant that we would never be able to spend anything on a night out, because Barcelona was far away and everything would go towards the mortgage. No surprises.

While running I know that:

Having our daughter was so extraordinary that I had to become conventional to bear witness to it. I no longer wanted to do dirty realism, I wanted to do clean folk art. My style of drawing changed because, of course, I wanted her to be excited about it. I wanted to draw for children. Some critics thought it terrible, thinking it was due to giving up nightlife; others thought it better, thinking that it was due to matrimonial stability. It was because of motherhood, but I didn't say so: that would have meant the end of good reviews. I could no longer be cynical. I was too scared. I stopped drawing busty women and nocturnal cities with bins and rats, and started drawing chickens in the oven and freshly baked cakes.

In the sex advice column of a magazine I read: 'Lastly, the most important thing of all: we must make lubricant our friend. We can use it as much as we wish. It must be water-based (Vaseline or oil-based products are aggressive to the vaginal pH). You can buy it in the pharmacy, the supermarket or on the internet. Try it! With this small change, you'll see how much more pleasurable and enjoyable your sexual relations will be'.

Making friends with lubricant. What fun.

A noise. I lift my head from the drawing of the untidy children's nursery I have to submit tomorrow and look around. My neighbour has thrown a little stone at the window, like Madame Bovary's lover. Our walls touch and the PVC windows face each other because his house — the last one on the corner — juts out more than the others. His study has a small balcony with a medium-sized flowerpot. There's a little kumquat tree on it.

I wave hello and he brings two fingers to his mouth to indicate smoking. I nod, and stick my head out the window.

'Hello,' I say.

'A fag and back to work?'

I only smoke when out for dinner, but I enjoy these breaks from time to time. I gave him a drawing of him writing and he's hung it up in there. Now he's requested a leave of absence from the school to write a new novel. He likes to read passages aloud to me.

His name is Carles Jordi, and I don't know anyone else with that name. His evasive style of writing makes him a very cheerful, lively man. Laughing men surprise me, master me, fascinate me. Nothing my neighbour writes brings his soul into question (maybe that's why he laughs) and I already know all the music my husband plays does (maybe that's why he doesn't laugh any more, among other reasons). He writes contemporary thrillers, with spies, tightly drawn political plots (corruption and journalism) and brave female protagonists (with this accepted female courage these days), always strong and determined, never a blonde, just in case. This hurts his wife, because the descriptions don't resemble her at all. Every day she works in a motor concession so, happily settled on leave in the meantime, he can describe ideal women that aren't like her and ignore those like her, because those like her can't be heroines in books, only readers of them. I know it hurts her, because one day I heard them arguing from home (my father would say the walls we have are 'paper-thin').

If these women he describes were male protagonists rather than female, they'd be something akin to Rambo. But since they're women, they can raise children, climb, be sensitive, love their excess weight, hack computers (they're always very talented in detecting security flaws in cyber companies) and have forgettable sexual encounters that never make them suffer or feel insecure. They always have witty comebacks at the ready. (No friendship with lubricant or pad for accidents). There's no longer any possibility of reading about women who aren't 'strong'. But what if you aren't strong? And no matter how much you search every fictional tale, every single one, you can't find any sort of redemption? What should what you'd like to read be called? New Contemporary Menopausal Literature, I suppose.

As the little one grew older (five, six, seven, eight ...) Neptune began to complain about the routine. He said he'd like to give up the private lessons and the engagements accompanying ballad singers in Andorra (this very well-paid work in Andorra came his way from time to time); if he could choose he'd rather not play in the orchestra, but do his own thing, be able to form the jazz quartet he always says he wants to, and that maybe now, at last, he'll do it with Cristina (a jazz quartet with two violins).

One day at my publisher, they suggested my illustrating an inconsequential non-fiction book written by a journalist about the advantages of making lists, and I said yes, to earn some quick cash and save him for a while from the engagements in Andorra and the evenings of spoiled brats with their little violins. Illustrating the book of lists was just another job, like making shower curtains with butterflies and beetles with their names (*Erebia medusa, Danaus plexippus* ...). Lists to make life better. Lists of intentions, of foods you shouldn't eat, of clothes you should throw away, of things you can do to make someone fall in love with you ...The drawings had to be 'modern' and 'elegant', with tall, thin women, well-dressed and glamorous, drinking cocktails with little umbrellas. And I had to do it with the same skill as the butterflies on the curtains.

Then the book of lists became a bestseller and topped all the lists; everyone was giving it as a present. And I was no longer a 'delicious' (that adjective was always applied to me) and 'sensitive' artist; I was the illustrator who'd done that nice lists crap, which indeed everyone found to have a 'very elegant' style. And of course everyone talked to me about the book of lists, not about the other things I'd illustrated without the said elegant style, and which no one remembered. The book of lists was translated into every language, but not my other things, like the monster ones for kids with such personal drawings. Everyone wanted the 'tag-team' made up of me and the author of the book of lists to do more things. A book about tidying when you're very messy, for example. I got the job doing the political cartoon strip in the newspaper (it goes without saying they preferred the drawing style from the book of lists). My colleagues no longer treated me as one of them, and with good reason. I'd crossed over to the 'commercial' side. Somehow Neptune resented that, and that's why — partly, but not only — he must fall in love with Cristina. He wouldn't have turned the list illustrator's liver into tinned foie-gras. But I was damned, whatever I did. I made the book of lists so that he could feel like more of an artist. If I hadn't done the book of lists, he'd have had to continue with the private lessons and the ballad singers in Andorra, and he wouldn't have felt like an artist. That would have made him sad and distant from me. Because I did do it, he'll be able to form a jazz quartet with Cristina and feel like an artist, but then, paradoxically, on the other hand, he won't think of me as one, merely the illustrator of the book of lists (and shower curtains and newspaper cartoon strips). This will embarrass him a little, and he'll fall in love with her: more of an artist than me, but one who couldn't give him the artist's life I do, which will make him distance himself from me.

While running I think:

When my mother died, exultant and abundant, my grand-mother did what fell to her and she'd already done when grandfather died: lighting candles, speaking softly, making incisive comments and crossing herself hastily, gracelessly, every time she finished a sentence. She took out my earrings and told me that from then on I must wear two black studs as a sign of mourning. She cut off my pigtails (my mother used to make me wear pigtails that looked like strings of sausages, with three hairbands top, middle and bottom) with the chicken scissors, because she couldn't do my hair (and I cried more about my hair than about my mother's death). When he saw me with my hair cut off and brushed back, my father said: 'Shit, you look like Shane!' He was referring to the cowboy character in the eponymous film; he'd let us watch the Alan Ladd series on TV. After his wife's death he was overcome by a state of idiotic confusion that would never leave him.

At school, the pity for my sorrow lasted for two classes; in no time they were laughing at my head, shorn like a mangy boy. Schools used to be what Twitter is now. Your mother dies and everyone sends their condolences, but how long does it take for the first joke to come?

The most important consequence of my mother's death was that I stopped fixing Tiet Ventura. I didn't do it on the day of the funeral (he stayed with a neighbour). Nor the next day. And on the third day, when my grandmother asked me to do it, I said no and ran away.

She begged me, she said her hands weren't strong enough and that she couldn't ask a man to do 'such a thing.' All in vain. Unfixed now, Tiet Ventura's shouts woke up the cows, who bellowed back, making the dogs bark at the same time. I'd made a perverse illustrated story of it, which I still have:

What does Tiet say? 'Hiiii!' [and a drawing of my uncle]

And how does the cow answer him? 'Moooo!' [and a drawing of the cow]

And how does the dog answer them? 'Woof-woof!' [and a drawing of the dog]

And what must we do to keep the cow and dog quiet?

Fix Tiet! [And a drawing of a little girl with a shorn head, fixing my uncle].

Our other bachelor uncle, Tiet Eusebi — Sebi — brother of my father and Tiet Ventura, lived with us on the farm. It was he who looked after the animals with my brother Felip (Father never did anything other than chatting to and flattering the women who used to come to buy eggs, milk or rabbits). Tiet Sebi used to shout: 'Do whatever you want!'

One orange-skied night, I asked my brother Felip to come with me to the hayloft, which was where we told each other secrets. 'I've put up with it for a long time, now it's your turn to put up with it,' I said. We both went to peep at Tiet Ventura, who was sitting in a chair in the dining room as always, his hands stiff on the sticky greasy tablecloth. Such a hateful, happy, needy roar when he saw me. I showed my brother how to do it. I told him: 'Now his dick will get big'. I felt superior. I took his hand to guide him. I told him: 'Like this, until the liquid comes out.' My brother took it, much more fascinated and much less practically minded than me. He understood, or maybe not yet, that it was pleasant for Tiet Ventura because maybe he already guessed, or maybe not, that he'd like it too. 'It must be done to him. It must be done every day so he doesn't scream,' I said. And also: 'But only once. And you have to hide from him, because if he sees you, he always wants it.'

I'd imagined him whimpering, fleeing to avoid doing it like me. In my head I'd imagined the scene of persecution. But it didn't go that way. My brother, who was much taller than me despite being a year younger, said: 'Bitch, slut.' I didn't know what *slut* meant; I only knew the boys at school used to call you that. 'Say it very fast: luts, luts, luts.' And he left. And as he was leaving I kept repeating: 'Slut-slut-slut-slut,' until finally it sounded like 'Luts-luts-luts'.

I tell Neptune I want to go outside, I want to get some air, and coughing, I walk — feverish, with no strength — to the local pharmacy to buy the incontinence pads. For the first time.

The automatic glass doors open as I approach. A festive opening. A Festive Overture.

But back at home, sitting on the toilet, I realise I can't wear those pads I crept out to buy like an incontinent sneak. In front of the pharmacist, whom I vaguely know, I pretended they weren't for me, but for an unspecified old (old, old) lady, like that well-preserved actress the ladies like so much who advertises a brand on telly. 'Do you have pads for an old lady?' I said, betraying myself and all the well-hydrated, attractive ladies of my generation.

So she gave me some, that there on the toilet I see are huge and humiliating, for someone laughing a few kilometres down the road, who no longer needs to pretend anything, who is no longer a mammal but a reptile. I can't wear this, I think, if I always wear leggings around the house like a young girl. Or like a psycho who thinks she's a young girl, who has no self-awareness, who's shocked by the grey when she's caught unawares and hasn't pulled her head back in photos. My ass will look like a duck's if I wear it.

Then he opens the bathroom door. He doesn't know I'm there, his sneaky incontinent wife, sitting on the toilet, with this new basic necessity in my hand. He looks over, confused.

'What are you doing?' he says. 'Has your period come?'

Incontinence pads don't have the same wrapping as the others, but he doesn't know that. He's never really looked at these things before.

'No, sometimes I like remembering it,' I say. No, I don't know why I said it. That lie just came out.

He looks at me, as if I have some kind of chronic fatigue. He feels sorry for me.

'No need to remember anything,' he murmurs.

It's pity, nothing more. The love he has emerges out of pity, out of habit. Nothing else. He can't give me the embrace full of love and worship that Dani, accustomed to women wanting to fight time, would give me. Used to the presents from them; used to touching the abdominals our husbands don't see or wouldn't value; used to understanding the happy sacrifice in all our lunges and squats. Who sends New Year messages to his clients, and in return receives beautiful, very expensive watches for running, bought behind their husbands' backs (he swaps them out depending on whether he's training one or the other) with thousands of advantages that Gretchen, Francina and I always envy: good, noble, childish envy, envy for objects and not the lives of others, the envy between friends who love you intensely, sincerely and circumstantially.

While running I think:

When we first met, in the beginning, when we hadn't publicly reproached one another for anything, or got in each other's way in the kitchen, or did we think we ever would, because in the kitchen we used to paw one another and it was impossible to think that one day, one of us two, would wait in fury for the other to shut the dishwasher so we could go by, we used to walk around Barcelona and I'd see us reflected in the window of some bookshop. Brahms' *A German Requiem* in my head like in an ad. I was surprised by the sight in those early days. 'This is us!' Him so big, me so small.

One day we met my first ex (if my man is the god Neptune, my first ex is a panda bear, with a two-tone black and white beard, a big bald head, small ears and a hairy body) in the cocktail bar where I always went with everyone, including him, and he jokingly said in front of him that he was jealous of this relationship, that I was more beautiful now than when we were a couple (it was true) and that this tattooed man wouldn't love me as much as I deserved. It was half a joke but my love hated him immediately, and from that day on he wanted nothing to do with him and well, I continued to see him very occasionally. He also hated all the men that — then — wanted to bed me. I was thirty-something. He was twenty-something. But now I'm fifty-something. He's forty-something. He's much more worn out than me and will save the little energy remaining in an alcohol-pickled liver to rehearse with Cristina. He wouldn't get off the sofa for me now. He's been barefoot longer than shod with me, while Cristina hasn't (yet) seen him in socks.

If I think about what I was for him, I love him. How from the first day he was already in love with my drawings, my dirty cartoon strips. The old book he gave me: *Psychology of Love and Courtship,* which cost a pittance but made me laugh so much. The first encounter: the coffee in a bar the following morning, because I had to go and draw, (and 'have to go' was so mysterious), and staying for lunch and dinner, and sleeping together again, and going back to that bar. I imagined prehistoric caves with him on guard so the other Neanderthals wouldn't steal me. How he liked the practical parts of my body: my breasts, my legs, my ass, my hands. It's not a joke, the hands thing, not the way they say 'I like your hands,' so you won't think all they like about you are your breasts or ass. He liked them in the same way as my ass (but my hands drew, of course). We lived for the moment, we made the most of every second. We'd say dirty words in a mythic way. 'I want your cunt,' he'd say, 'or I will die.' 'I am in need of your dick,' I'd say. Everything we did — eat dinner, rest, drink, summarise and redesign our biographies — had a sexual undertone. Over the following days I began to put off my sometime lovers (I was living the life of a single girl and had lovers, one married) and he began to hide from his girlfriend, the one who saw Mozart coming yet didn't see me.

While running I remember:

After my mother's death, my father always used to say: 'I wasn't born for farm life. I was born to live the high life.' Sometimes, he would take the money from the biscuit tin (the money from selling eggs, rabbits and milk, which we used for everyday expenses) and say: 'I'll be back soon.' And he'd go to the bar and come back drunk. It was strange because when he was drunk he always seemed much smaller, like he'd shrunk. One night he didn't come back and Tiet Sebi discovered the notes he kept in the inside pocket of a blazer were also gone. We didn't see him again.

Infern de l'americana. Infern, hell, is the word for inside pocket in Catalan. Is it said this way in other languages?

Cristina's debut concert is in two weeks, before Sant Jordi on April 23rd. Normally they only rehearse three times the week before. A reading on Monday evening, playing all day on Wednesday, maybe going back for a half-day on Thursday, and performing Friday evening. Sometimes the musicians know the programmes very well and they've got it in a very short time. But he has wanted to work there every day, before the first reading. Every day! They'd know the score by heart, turn the minims into crotchets, the quavers into semiquavers, play at top speed without *faking* and lead.

· With each rehearsal, he'll fall more in love.

While running I can't get out of my head:

In a piece I entered in a school contest, I drew a very detailed comic about a young girl who had to fix her twisted uncle. The central part showed the bombardment (in black and white, copied somewhat from the classic Spanish comic *Hazañas bélicas*) that had left him in that state, and I'd heard my grandfather describe a thousand times. I was the best artist in the school. Every year I won a prize in that contest (once I won a Catalonia-wide contest, sponsored by a yoghurt brand). I can't say whether I was or wasn't expecting what would happen. I can't say whether I did it so they would take us out of there or it never occurred to me that they would do so. The truth is that the jury must have been horrified to see a penis in such detail, so well done, taking up two whole panels. They made me go to the headteacher's office (I thought it was because I'd won) and shuddering, they asked me where it had come from and what it meant. I don't remember what I said, it's been wiped from my memory, but I do remember we were taken to a child protection unit and my brother saw it as a betrayal. He liked the farm. I didn't, not at all. 'What have you done, bitch, slut?' he said. 'You're to blame, they're taking us away now because of everything you did to our uncle.' Many days he didn't go to school, but stayed helping Tiet Sebi. The animals came over to him as if he were St Francis of Assisi. He loved dogs, rabbits, pigeons, sparrows stripped of their nests, a squirrel that appeared one day. They all ate from his hand or mouth. He named the cows and the pigs, hunted flies and threw them into webs so spiders could sneakily go and find them. He is a bachelor now, without any human being around (he doesn't trust them), because it will only and ever be an animal that awakens his love and desire. He also said: 'You're like Papa, you are.' Luts-luts-luts.

What I remember about the child protection unit — the unit to us — is that he was crying and I wasn't. I was fascinated by the vibrant colours of the sheets and bedspreads: blue, purple and pink with lions and cats in circus costumes. In our house we had brown sheets with a mandrake pattern and yellowing pillowcases that were washed only very occasionally. Those colours. So comfortable, so irrelevant, so logical, so ancient. Someone had considered the fact that children like colours. I had to draw them, lions and cats like those. I wanted to do that job. Drawing bedspreads.

While running I recall:

When the little one was born and we had her in the pram, and we were isolated from the world, something happened to me that had never happened to me before. I'd never been exactly 'faithful' to any man. Never completely, even when I was. Was promiscuous singledom really my natural state of being — the flirting, the pursuit, the inability to miss a single, even theoretical, opportunity? I was one of those women who frightened other women, because I sympathised with their husbands, I understood them; a sexual mania that everyone would attribute to my background (and to avoid interpretations, I've never explained my background to anyone, not even Neptune).

Before him, with my previous husbands, I found it embarrassing to say 'my man'. I used to go to illustration conferences, fairs, and my body language was that of a 'single woman'. I didn't want to have children with the other two.

Now for all these years with him, I've been completely faithful. Even in my thoughts. I've never thought about anyone else. I've never even made jokes about men — as you sometimes see women do when they talk about actors or singers. Perhaps I simply haven't seen them because of my defective vision and didn't know they were there.

By contrast, in all this time with him, like all women, I wasn't short of offers, slimy or naive, attentive, filthy, begging, too daring or not daring enough. I've seen myself discarding opportunities; being faithful not by force but with temptation within reach. Like someone who doesn't drink at a party.

I used to go to the bookshop to buy a comic and when I got back, happy and amazed, I'd think: 'Great! I can tell him the truth. I went to buy a comic book. It's not an excuse!' I'd go for a drink with a colleague or my second ex (whom he doesn't hate as much as the first) or with a young, ambitious, persistent Fine Arts student, and when I came home I'd tell him the truth: 'I went for a drink with a colleague,' 'with my second ex,' 'with a young, ambitious, persistent Fine Arts student'. 'I went running' (the activity that's taken up the most time these last few years) and it was the truth. I mean I had no desire to deceive him. I'd leave my phone on the backrest of the sofa and think: 'I'll leave my phone there, I've got nothing to hide.' No one knew how sweet it was except me. I've never told him, because he wouldn't understand. Hiding weighs on you. It's a dog's life when you're hiding. I felt so rested by not hiding and no one could understand what it meant to rest because no one had hidden as much as me in the past. 'I have nothing to hide, nothing to hide, nothing to hide,' I'd repeat to myself. I didn't have to pretend I'd gone to the supermarket when I'd actually met up with another man to give him a fleeting, risky kiss, or wanted to call him for a moment from a phone box. That's what I did in my second marriage. Other than the first three years, lying all the while and going to phone boxes. When I cheated on my second husband very few people had mobile phones and having lovers was much more home-spun. I always say to Gretchen and Dani: 'You don't know how lucky you cheaters are with mobile phones.'

My whole life is a gallop between the pretentious and the epic, depending only on how many drinks I've had. If I don't drink alcohol, the world is rigid and predictable. I have energy in spades. I'm more creative (drink or no drink, I always run well), but I lack transcendence. If I don't drink, I clean the kitchen, I resemble a domestic goddess, I put on my pyjamas. But I can't be that way in front of him. I can't put up a fight in thick pyjamas. He loves (used to love) me sitting on a wine bar stool, in heels, talking about painting, recognising all the names of all the bottles of wine in the transparent wine fridge, knowing what song is playing in the background with no doubt at all, watching the night fall. If I want him not to love me, all I have to do is ask him to buy vacuum bags. If I want him to love me, I have to destroy myself.

'Today, I'm going to Cris' when rehearsal's over,' he tells me this afternoon.

I no longer have a fever, just a nasty cough (and its consequence) and feel a little bit weak. I'm stunned for a moment. I'm more shaken by the diminutive than the information. 'Cris'. Cris, so familiar.

'Buy vacuum bags if you can,' I reply.

All flustered and remorseful and sore, I call the dog. She has a funny name, the same as a dog famous in the world of comics, a considered name, from a complacently happy, somewhat urban family. I won't say it. I find it embarrassing now, because it no longer has any meaning. One of those ironic names. That's what we do. You name the fish Einstein and the turtle, Marie Curie (because, just as in the textbooks I illustrate, we must strive for gender parity in science). Francina's pair of hamsters are named after the King and Queen of Spain. We do things like that.

Anticipating her happiness, I show her the leash, and we go out to pick up the little one from her extra-curricular theatre class in the town civic centre. I imagine them both in the Gràcia flat (the street is Ros de Olano, I now know) and I 'see' the flat. Like when you unconsciously imagine the house of someone you know that you've never seen. A work colleague says, self-deprecatingly, that he fell asleep on the sofa watching football and even if you've never seen his house, you see it without realising; you 'visualise' the sofa and tv, maybe not with total clarity. And if you finally see his house one day, your brain automatically focuses on the real sofa and you forget what you had created forever. With Cristina I see a chest of drawers (maybe found in a skip) painted off-white and then sanded, with a collection of very red lipsticks on top, and I also see a coat rack with many felt hats bought at flea markets.

Cris. If he called her 'Cris' in front of me, he's clearly already calling her 'Cris'. But what was it like the first time?

I buy the little one a Calippo and go to a park with zip-wires so she can eat it sitting down, because we like to give some to the dog and laugh at her surprise at the ice. I check WhatsApp to see if he's said anything, and as he's not said anything (he never says anything), I send him a photo of the little one with the Calippo. What ridiculous, petty blackmail.

'Where's Papa?'

'At Cristina's house, rehearsing.'

'Oh.'

'Papa thinks it's better that she doesn't always have to go back and forth on the train, poor girl,' I explain.

But it doesn't seem strange to her, or at least she doesn't show it.

A piece of her Calippo falls on the ground. Suddenly three or four little kids that were playing in the sand pit come running with their plastic spades. Without a word, they bury the piece of ice cream in the sand. A moment of coordination. Three spadefuls and it's already underground. They pat the sand with their spades to compact it. Why did they want to bury it, why? And once done, they leave as quickly as they came, going back to the sandpit. My daughter watches them with the amused superiority of an elder. I don't, I see them as monsters with a secret mission. I'm afraid of these kids.

'Come on, let's go, let's run,' I say. Cris, Cris, Cris.

While running I think about him, him, now:

For me now, he's like one of those radio announcers you listen to absently every day. They have tics that you know well and maybe find irritating that no longer surprise you; you criticise them, you laugh at them, but if they were to call it a day and be replaced by another announcer, you'd be sorry because you'd come to miss them. If he were to leave, what I'd come to miss in him most would be a gesture he makes while tuning. He puts the violin on his shoulder and holds it with his chin alone. He does this to show that it needn't be held with his hand, that his hand makes no effort. It must be free for its dance of fingers.

I'm completely fine, but the cough doesn't go away. The good weather arrives; it's not long until Sant Jordi. I'm going to Barcelona to sign the book of lists and my neighbour the one about these strong women. I'm full of energy again and I celebrate it as if it were a superpower, but I'm someone else. I'm an old woman and I'll never again be what I was. Gretchen, Dani, Francina and I go out running in the morning after dropping the girls off at school, and we do our dozen kilometres on the mountain with the dogs, surrounded by almond and olive trees. A farmer has put out lots of little bottles of water, upside down, along the wire enclosing the field.

'You have to go to the doctor. That cough isn't normal,' says Francina. The cough is so much a part of my body now, so much so that I can't understand why the others don't have it too.

'It's a nervous cough; put an onion under your bed,' says Gretchen.

'It's an unproductive cough,' says Dani.

Coughing, I promise them I'll go to the GP. A reproductive happiness is perceptible in the atmosphere. Insects, birds, each one of them accepting the age that is their lot, doing what is their lot, reproducing without alcohol and without Beethoven, kicking out their chicks; no excuse, then, to continue partially keeping up that nest without young.

'Go on in front, if you want,' says Gretchen to Dani. She doesn't like to run fast on descents.

'No way! I can't go faster, it jerks the knees,' he goes.

We're always so kind to each other. Often the time we spend running will contain the most kindness of our whole day and night.

'I had a fight with my wife last night,' Francina murmurs.

'Explain,' Gretchen shouts from the front.

And all three of us ready ourselves to listen and understand, as usual, as every day.

'Sometimes she makes me the mother and sometimes she makes me the daughter,' she complains.

'I know what you mean,' I say.

We all listen to her short explanation, which will never go any further.

Phase 1: You put your feet in between his because you're cold. He's proud, he wants to look after you.

Phase 2: You put your feet in between his because you're cold. He jokingly complains a little.

Phase 3: You don't put your feet in between his, even though you're cold, so he won't think you want sex.

Phase 4: If by mistake you put your feet in between his, there's no chance either will think the other wants sex.

Phase 5: Separate beds due to snoring, sickness, hatred or insomnia. If there's money and few prejudices, separate rooms. If not, very often one of the two (in a heterosexual relationship it's usually him) sleeps on the sofa.

Phase 6: The death of one of the two and the sweet longing of the other.

All this, of course, without counting on the entrance of a Cristina. If so, you skip over Phases 5 and 6 and he returns to Phase 1.

I illustrated lists like this one for the journalist's book of lists, but they weren't so sad.

While running I remember:

While we were in the child protection unit our grandmother had an attack of apoplexy (that's what they used to call a stroke before, too) and then Tiet Sebi hired a woman from the town to keep house and wash Tiet Ventura. (I don't know whether he asked her to fix him). We knew her. Her name was Quima and she always went around with so many oil-stains that the town kids used to call her the 'filthy woman'. But it seems that he, well over forty and never having known a woman, fell in love with her. He wrote her a card in which he asked for her hand in marriage. I have it, because it stayed there, crumpled up, once the apparently laughing woman turned him down, and my grandmother picked it up.

That same day, the day he was turned down, Tiet Sebi ate the lentil stew made by her; he had a coffee, also made by her; he left the animals mating, made straight for the hayloft, covered his head with an oat sack and shot himself with the hunting rifle. My grandmother found him. My brother went to the funeral. I didn't. I was afraid they might catch me again, make me stay with them, and I wanted the unit. The children's books in the unit, the carers in the unit, the vibrant sheets in the unit. I pretended that I was too badly affected, and everyone understood and asked me to do some drawing, how nice it was feeling understood and making drawings there. Making drawings to avoid talking. How could I not have wanted to be an illustrator. 'You're like Papa'.

Tiet Sebi wrote the letter in Spanish, the language learnt at school, the prestigious one, but there's a sentence he didn't know how to translate that remained in Catalan, there among all the formalities like 'Esteemed Quima, I write herein to tell you that ...' The line is: (with errors corrected): '*M'he agradat de vostè i li duc voluntat*'. I admire you and I am at your service. What is surprising is that he wrote the whole letter in capitals, except this sentence in lower-case. Why? Because he unconsciously considered this other language to be a minor one, forbidden by the dictatorship, not studied at school? Or because he vaguely guessed the idea of italics, of quotation marks, of the distinction between the two? Because then it means that from the beginning of the letter he'd known he would write this — to him untranslatable — sentence. *I admire you*. So utterly sad.

The following day is Saturday, and Cristina comes to rehearse the whole morning in an ankle-length dress that shows off her neckline and hides her hips. Let's just say that the evening my love went to rehearse in Ros de Olano he came back loathing the discomfort. There was no grand piano or pipe to smoke or whisky or any of the comforts of a married man there.

She has beautiful eyes, Cristina — grey and a little tearful. I can see her underwear, squeezing the cheeks of an ass unfamiliar with Body Pump, muscle stiffness, Dani's jokes. I imagine her at our communal pool, her legs covered in cellulite. Because of sport I have very little, only on my ass. But my knees are already all saggy. Who would want to kiss them?

'I like your dress,' I tell her. I go to the toilet so often to change my incontinence pad that I worry he'll think I'm a cokehead.

If I'd said 'You're very pretty,' he would have suspected me. I never say things like that to women in front of him. So far we were neck and neck.

'Really? It's African.'

She tells me the story of the dress, where she bought it (somewhere in Gràcia, of course) and when. So young she seems, so proud with her hips, so infuriating and arrogant. I listen to her with the interest of a friend of her mother's. What am I intending? I suppose today I vaguely know.

'Do you want to have lunch and then rehearse?' I ask.

I'm playing mother. All of a sudden he and she are the children. The same thing that's happening to Francina. To everyone.

'Yes, maybe,' he says.

'Something simple?' I insist.

'Make a green salad and I'll go and buy a rotisserie chicken, if you like,' he says.

Green salad is the only dish he accepts I can prepare without making a mistake (and even so he very often criticises the excess or lack of salt and vinegar).

I'm laughing inside. What will she do? Will she stay with me, slowly chopping tomatoes and carrots, with the absurd thoroughness and inefficiency of a guest, trying to make conversation, or will she go with him to the rotisserie shop? Which course will be chosen? 'Oh you, sliced carrots?' or 'Oh you, chicken turning on the spit?'

The little one is playing on the tablet, and I call her to set the table. Cristina wants to help too, and I try to refuse, 'No, no, no need Cristina, I'm doing it.' People asking where things are sets me on edge. 'Where are the glasses?' They always ask for specific things that I don't know whether we have (I have), like 'Do you have a platter?' 'Do you have a serrated knife?' I don't know, I'm a gnome, ask me for spells to pull snakes out of your mouth.

'I'll come with you and we'll split the cost,' she says ('Oh you, chicken turning on the spit ...!')

'No!' he protests. 'I'm paying. But yes, come with me and that way we'll listen to the recording in the car.'

'We'll listen to the recording in the car.' That hurts me, I admit. They've recorded it on their mobile phones and now they'll connect it to the speakers (or something similar beyond my understanding). I feel replaced. But I immediately go back to being the mild queen mother, the duchess of incontinence.

While running I think:

Years ago, when the little one was in nursery, I went to pick her up with a brightly coloured beach bag I'd designed for the bedspreads, shower curtains and tablecloths company. She looked at it and looked at it again, felt it, and the moans she was making and her manner of examining the texture were clearly an aesthetic feeling. A kind of pre-school Stendhal syndrome. I always moan too, I can't help it. I moan when I run, I moan in bed, I moan with joy or sorrow, while asleep, after an effort at the gym; I always moan. It's the sound that defines me. I could dub porn while I shower, eat or fold laundry. She'll never remember the thing with the bag. She'll not be able to remember the moment she had to touch a thing to understand it. She can't remember that sincerity and feeling for painting, for colours, which she won't re-discover until she's my age. As is well-known, at my age the sun coming up would make you applaud.

We sit at the kitchen table. Him in his spot; me in mine, on his left; the little one in hers, on the right. Cristina in the one that's free, which belongs to no one (because its back is to the telly). He carves the chicken, a job reserved for the husband. He knows I like thighs, he gives me a thigh. He knows the little one likes breasts, so he gives her a breast. What does Cristina like? We'll soon know.

'It's all the same to me, anything is fine,' she says.

'A wing, then. That's the best part,' he says.

The little one and I look at each other. He always tries to get us to eat wings, but he never succeeds. He succeeds with Cristina, because she's new. Cristina goes along with him in everything. She sits on his left and turns the page.

Afterwards I go make coffee (a job reserved for the wife). Time to find out how Cristina takes it, listen to her precise explanation. Maybe she wants black coffee because she ... Maybe she doesn't take sugar because she's ... Maybe she prefers tea and I'll have to dig out a teapot from the cupboards? No. I'm not making tea. I'll say we don't have any.

'Do you have stevia?' she asks me.

'No. What is it?'

She looks at me with happy smugness.

'Wow, how funny. Just there you reminded me of my mother,' she tells me with a magnificent smile.

Not one muscle in my face moves. I swear I am considering the possibility of killing her. There's a great system: in fact, I don't know why more people don't kill this way. Drink lots of alcohol, a lot, and knock her down one evening when she comes out of our house to go catch the train (soon he won't bring her even to the station any more).

'No, not like that, I mean it in a good way,' she adds. 'My mother is a marvellous lady.'

My mother wasn't. That is why I am. Hers is. That's why she's not.

Turn myself in to the police straightaway so they do the breathalyser and it comes back positive. Very positive, not just a tiny bit positive. Say I don't remember what happened. Say I don't have a driving licence, I don't know what came over me. I wouldn't go to prison. It would be that easy. No more than a matter of accelerating and being able to bear bits of brain mixed with locks of pink-coloured hair on the windscreen. But I'd also have to bear his sorrow, and that would indeed be unbearable.

While having lunch, an indignant Cristina told us that Von Karajan didn't want women in the orchestra. And me?

I met my first husband when I legally left the unit. Like my father, I washed my hands of my brother, my uncle, my stroke-ridden grandmother. I pretended they weren't there. I began making my own way as if I were an orphan. Along with my other comrades, all released at eighteen, we went to France to work in the grape harvest. We bought diet pills containing amphetamines with fake prescriptions in the pharmacy and resold them for more money to those who wanted to invest (they were banned after a while). We sneaked onto the train, hiding ourselves in the toilet, without bolting it shut, so the conductor (who everyone nicknamed the 'clippie') would think there was no one in there. The things we did.

Through one of these comrades (the son of a servant named Visitación, *Visi,* whom the master had praised to the skies) I got work helping to set up the dressing rooms for a concert organised by Amnesty International at Barcelona's Montjuïc stadium. We had to put sofas, tables and chairs in the musicians' trailers, staple carpets and, of course, I painted murals on the dressing room doors and symbols of witches and wizards on the toilets. He was the concert promoter and a minor celebrity in the world of management. He was sixteen years older than me, and since he rescued me from the streets, I conveniently ignored the fact that he went to bed with all the singers and chorus girls he promoted as well as with me. He gave me a job: I was to decorate his bars in Ibiza. We got married there.

I didn't fall in love with him, I fell in love with (adult) protection: work, clothes, alcohol, tubes and tubes of paint, the vinyl records he gave me and the flat (with a cinema room, erotic photographs on the headboard of the bed and the biggest library I'd ever seen). He enrolled me in the university and there I began to get my first jobs: a poster for a town's annual festival, another for a fishmonger's (with sea snails, lobsters and a mermaid) ... Then a well-known illustrator came to the department saying he was looking for a colourist (the person who does panel backgrounds) for a cartoonist. The job, which would last for two years, was mine (and after a few years he ended up being my second husband). He'd draw the characters and I'd do the 'background': he, the bad guy shooting out of a car window; me, the lampposts, the trees, the moon, the cats in front of buildings. I learnt everything I know from him, but soon I learnt things he no longer wanted to know too, because he was also older than me and jaded. Two years of colouring backgrounds, not sleeping at night when I had to deliver, happy because I was making a living from illustration, even though the colourist's signature wasn't on the work. Being a colourist was a way of being: mine. I preferred the stuffing to the meat, the garnish to the slice.

When the book was published, some tv people did a feature on the author and I appeared on screen too, on the side, cleaning brushes. When my father saw me, he called the publisher and left a phone number, which turned out to be that of a bar.

'Hey Shane, I saw you on tv!' he said when I called back. 'You must have cash now.'

We met in a pizzeria on the Gran Via called El Viejo Pop, which had a bearded hippy riding a bicycle as its logo. He said he was living with a woman, Cati, who took jobs in houses. 'Don't think the worst of her, she makes a very good living.' Then he let me know he had debts with a moneylender. If I didn't want his legs broken in three places (a hat-trick, he said), I had to give him money, which he'd give back straightaway once he closed a deal he was making with some entrepreneurs who wanted to invest in Gabon. To invest in Gabon, he had to become a Knight of the Order of Malta and he needed money for the uniform. I didn't even know where Gabon was and, baffled by the intricacy of the lie, I gave him money, which then was still counted in pesetas.

About six months later he went to prison for fraud and I found out that Cati was actually a prostitute (luts). I never visited him in prison. My brother did. I saw no one. First my grandmother died ('Kids, don't go see who's dead, because it's me!'), then Tiet Ventura, and I didn't even know. My brother took care of them.

While running I think:

The fact of wanting to draw extraordinary stories makes my existence extremely banal. On the other hand, when I draw banal things, like the lists, whether I like it or not, my existence is more extraordinary.

But last year, my father got out of prison and pre-menopausal me lost the fury I felt; I thought he might die, and I wanted him to get to know Neptune and the little one. We settled on the idea that he'd come for lunch once a month with my in-laws (whom I loved so much, because they were *so normal*) and we'd give him money. My father lived with Cati and a son of hers in a flat on Carrer Hospital, a street in central Barcelona. My brother was a shepherd. I called him too, but he's never forgiven me for the time spent in the unit. 'You're a bitch and you wanted me to be a swine.'

'Spend the day.' So now my father and my in-laws come and 'spend the day' one Sunday every month. Spend the day. You can only say this old-fashioned phrase if you expect a natural order to life; if you don't know that your man is falling in love with another woman; if you don't expect much, really.

bC, he would go to pick them up from the station in the car and make cannelloni or salt-baked fish or roast lamb (these Sunday kinds of things). But since today she's also here rehearsing (it makes me laugh that after so many rehearsals a man in a cape will come and direct them in a requiem mass), we're going to have roasted chicken again, like the ones I so happily draw, and all three are coming, my father and my in-laws, on foot, limping from the station, like an old-time comedy troupe, over-pleasant and over-careful. My mother-in-law is shod as if she'll always have to have a man beside her to give her his arm. She envisions herself this way, holding an arm, because she's one of those women who believe — they say — 'they don't know how to walk in flats'. My love studied in the music conservatory because his mother loves music (she says she could have been a soprano), unlike his father, who has neither an ear nor a feeling for music. Of all of us, it's she who loves it most. Then me, before him, but not before Cristina, who is more moved than anyone when she plays. I could never draw again, but I would always want music.

We let the morning go by, sitting there in twenty-euro outdoor chairs, greying from heavy rain, on the strip of artificial grass that came with the house, trying to make conversation. The little one is looking at Tik Tok upstairs, and he and Cristina at scores in the basement. At twelve on the dot we have a vermouth, as is right and proper. For me, life would be like this: a perpetual aperitif, nothing too deep, finding everything good in a simple way, grazing, not chewing too much, hearing the so-stimulating crunch of the crisps, alcohol on an almost empty stomach, salt, no appetite for lunch and finally, not having lunch.

My father sips the brine straight from the tin of cockles. I uncork bubbly for myself and my mother-in-law because he wants a vermouth (a teeny vermouth) 'but in a glass, with no frills'. I put crisps in a bowl, with no flourishes (I don't know what to do now that Neptune has left these administrative tasks I find so embarrassing to me) and he grabs the bag and doesn't let it go.

At lunch time (a long hour later) everyone comes to the kitchen. We don't have a dining table (my mother-in-law always scolds us about that) because we have the grand piano in the very small living room. Sofa and piano, or sofa and table, it couldn't fit everything. When we first had the house, when we'd so happily decided not to have a table, we'd made some dinner, just the two of us (we could be alone and we wanted to be) with the plates on top of the piano. The little one was a baby, watching us from her Maxi-Cosi.

My father has brought two hundred and fifty grams of serrano ham in a little packet. Without even asking for a plate he throws it on the table, and tells us what it came to: thirty euro. He looks at my mother-in-law:

'I said "give me an ass of serrano ham", know what I mean, an ass?'

The woman says yes, with the disheartened, stupefied, reproachful and over-polite expression she always gives him, yes, she knows what an ass means.

'And he cut the remnants for me.'

He very often uses words I don't recognise. Words that will be lost when he dies.

It's my father-in-law who immediately takes the reins of the conversation. He always wants to please me, and he succeeds, because I adore repetition and banality, the inconsequential, the rise and fall of voices. He wants to please me more than my father and my man. My mother-in-law looks at Cristina, who can't resist the ham, and her eyes show that she understands.

'You've lost weight, girl,' she tells me.

'Not at all!' I protest. But I'm grateful for her words.

Cristina has this feigned, overdone desire to listen to the elderly of young people wanting to be 'unique'. Everything my father-in-law says is 'amazing', everything my mother-in-law declares is 'absolutely' and my father, licking his fingers and running them over the inside of the crisp packet, is 'amusing'.

'There's something I wanted to tell you, for your work,' my father-in-law says to me.

The man always worked at night, in a printer's. Retired now, it's as if he's discovering the sunlight, the pleasures of gossip, daytime insects and children awake, shops and, of course, being heard. He's one of those men with the quirk of liking trains — they still exist. Their anxieties about their worth and their artistic bent have come to rest here: trains. Why trains, and not planes or cars? No one knows. They have a lot in common, trainspotters. They're neat, often with a little moustache, they pay their taxes, they comb their hair back and put cologne on their heads, they stroll to buy the newspaper, they wear wine-coloured woollen vests.

'You already know your man's grandfather was at Saint-Cyprien and from there in the San Sebastián bullring. Has he told you about that or not? Have you told her about it, Òscar?'

So present in their lives, the war. Making war. Playing soldiers. Like a game. Actually, like his wife and daughter, Neptune doesn't know him well, because he was always sleeping. He's a friendly stranger who annoys them now, being awake.

'Yes, I think so,' he says. But he's never told me anything about it.

'He backed a guy who paid five gold coins to get him out of there.'

My father is licking his fingers, like a large monkey with an intelligent but absent expression.

'Well, this guy, who was very influential, was a friend of the bishop of Barcelona. His name was Díaz de Gomara,' my father-in-law goes on.

He believes it to be important, he wants me to take an interest and speak to the newspaper people (he thinks they'd listen to me), giving me lots of details that don't appear to be made up. He wouldn't tell me about it if he didn't know for certain what happened to this bishop. I say yes, and I would have died of love if it hadn't been for what I already know. Cristina opens her eyes so wide I worry they'll fall into the dish, like the paintings of St Lucy with her eyes on a plate, but she ignores me. She must think the illustrator of the book of lists isn't a worthy depository of this memory from her future love's father.

'My aunt was a doorkeeper in Sant Sever church. Her husband had been killed in the Sant Elies cheka.'

'You've already told this story, they already know ...' says my mother-in-law. She's spent her whole life giving singing lessons with her husband in bed, not at the table for a single meal, and it bothers her that he wants to make up for lost time now.

There's the audible sound of a woodpecker in a tree. It vibrates like my watch for running, which tells me when my heart rate rises: tock tock tock tock tock.

'Have I already told this? Do you already know about it?' Cristina comes to the rescue.

'I don't! I don't know about it…' In a little-girl voice. It sounds like 'I blee know about blah …'

She's been heedlessly drinking the bubbly and it's obvious. She wants to please his father, and for him to perceive it.

'They were taken in the *auto de la muerte,* "death car", to the Montcada i Reixac cemetery …'

'Man, they must have been total rebels,' exclaims my father. Not a reproach or a eulogy, that word: *rebels.* He talks about them as if he were talking about anyone's fate. Bucolic.

I look at her. Cris, Cristina. She has a pretty name, one for a wanted daughter. I have an ugly name, after the saint of the day, for an unwanted daughter. Remei. Like medicine, remedy. Francina calls me Mei, a disguise that had never occurred to me. I don't like those who call me Reme without asking. We call her Fran, but Francina seems like a pretty name to me.

'Well, my aunt, who did religious embroidery, used to monogram the bishop's underwear. And when he was killed, it was she who had to go and identify him by his underwear. 'Yes, yes, these are his underpants,' she said. 'A. P. Antonio Ponti.' She went to identify them at the Hospital Clínic. Him and two others. Can't you get an interview out of this?'

As if the monkey has heard a noise, my father raises his head. He's already finished licking the bag and with a finger he stirs his vermouth (with a cube of ice and an olive in it).

'I have stories too, you know,' he protests. 'I also have things to tell you if you want to make one of those weird illustrated books; a book that's out of the ordinary …' He takes a breath. 'I had a cousin who caught that disease when you don't eat.'

I smile. Cristina is like those television journalists I've seen performing outside of work: they're able to feign an over-the-top, gormless interest in anything, but for a maximum of three minutes. Then, their enthusiasm wanes. She's already tired of it.

'Shall I clear the table for you, girl?' asks my mother-in-law. 'Today we didn't remember to bring the usual cake.'

'Hang on, why you? Why the women?' Cristina complains, but laughing.

'That's true.' Serious, Angèlica agrees with her.

'For you'. The indirect object. She uses it without realising, in the same way she says to her husband 'Buy washing machine detergent for me'. 'For me.' It's suddenly funny to think what will happen if the lady starts sweeping and wiping things with a dust cloth in front of Cristina and serves the men a whisky once she has them take off their shoes.

Anyhow, she clears it (for me).

My father stretches out on one of the twin folding chairs, bought at the DIY store; he closes his eyes and is snoring within a minute, something that completely dismantles any theories about insomnia and regrets. My father-in-law paces up and down nervously. Cristina has put a scarf on her hair, taken off her sweater and sits in a khaki top, sunbathing and above all showing off her intense enjoyment. She wouldn't have done it with no audience. From my fifty-something years I look at her. How long do I have before morbid punctuality, before scolding drivers at pedestrian crossings, before a lack of thirst, before a desire to overeat and put cologne on my hair? How long before self-help and personal growth? Before flower-arranging courses? Before abandoning slang and technology? Before sending very late, very fake warnings to all my WhatsApp groups? Before sunbathing, not like she is, but for purely medical reasons?

After twenty minutes, when we've judged the nap to have been a success, my love announces that it's time to rehearse. My father gets up (a stiff, rigid movement, like Dracula rising from his coffin).

'You, Shane. Let's not wait too long before seeing each other, time might run out if we take too long, eh?' he says, jokingly, as if he means he'll die.

And straightaway he rubs his thumb and index finger together, making the stereotypical gesture for 'money'.

'Won't you show me a little affection today Shane?' he pesters me.

I already have an envelope prepared, which I give him in full view of everyone, so it's clear we both do it for money.

'If you want, I'll take you to the station,' my man says.

But no one could say yes to this conditional offer.

'No, no need, son, leave it, leave it,' says my mother-in-law. 'This way we'll digest our lunch.'

'Angèlica, come and say goodbye,' I shout.

It's been some time since the little one slipped away upstairs, sneakily, so no one would notice. No one in this house is on sure ground except me.

They meekly put on their jackets. My father is saying to my mother-in-law:

'Yesterday they had a film at the cinema that I didn't like. And I said: 'You know what? Go to hell!'

While running I wonder:

If I could, would I make it so that Cristina had never appeared in our lives?

Yes.

Why?

Because of the fear of everyone's gossip when they find out. Because of not having foreseen this ending. Because of my mother-in-law's sorrow. To avoid seeing how my little one prefers her to me and tells me nice things about her with a touch of cruelty.

Could I stop him falling in love with her if I try harder?

No.

Would I try if I could stop it?

Probably not.

Could I stop him going to bed with her if I demand he cut her out of our lives?

Maybe.

Do I want him to continue to love me as much as ever?

Yes. No. I want to float along, no more. I want him to be frozen.

Do I want to have sexual relations with him?

I can't say yes, I can't say no. But I wouldn't want him having them with anyone else.

Do I want to have them with someone else?

No. No.

Alone?

No.

Are there people in the world who want to have them with me?

Yes.

Should I think about these people? State your reasons for the answer.

Yes. Because doing it with them would be redemption and sacrifice all at once.

Should I think about those who have gone to bed with me? State your reasons for the answer.

Yes. I should forgive my first ex (without him realising). I should ask for forgiveness from my second ex (without him realising). I should get them together one last time (without them realising).

'I want to throw a party for Sant Jordi this year,' I say to my love that evening. 'To celebrate our anniversary. After a whole day signing, which is funny, because this year ...'

He and I met each other on the night of Sant Jordi, at my publisher's party, when I hadn't the faintest idea I'd end up illustrating any book of lists. I'd just won a prize for my first comic; one of those prestigious books that don't sell at all. He was playing in a quartet of jazz standards, put together expressly for that day. They didn't even rehearse. They played while people ate canapés and drank cava, and I went over and complimented them.

'Oh yes? But who do you mean? There's no one nearby ...'

He smiles a hollow, exhausted smile. He's not into parties. We no longer have to show ourselves off to the world.

'My running friends ... parents from school, people from the newspaper ... Jordi ...' Jordi is my second ex. 'People from the orchestra, if you like; our neighbour ...'

'Well, it all depends on how many people it would be, no?'

'Cristina too,' I add.

'Yes, yes, of course.'

I want to dance with a glass in my hand after spending all day signing the book of lists in Barcelona. And that night, at the party, be inwardly grateful for it all and take action, because if I don't hurry, I won't be in time. Not for leaving, nor for telling him to leave, nor for fighting (nor for killing her, for killing him, for killing myself).

bC, when I got home from drawing the newspaper cartoon strip (I do it in the editorial department there, because they help me choose the subject or I wouldn't be able to do it), everything would stop. He, the little one and the dog would come out to meet me and try to gauge my mood, which was very important to them. There were good, homey things like grilled calamari, chicken skewers (bought ready-made, to put straight into the pan), vegetable soup. Everyday things. Mashing tender green beans and potatoes with a fork. Doing this for a long time so the bean ends up completely mashed. Turning it into a paste and once done constructing a kind of plateau on top used to make me bellow quietly inside from solitary happiness. The little one would grumble while I did it. I'd think: 'How happy I am, how happy I am … I don't want to be anyone else.'

But everything changed, from one day to the next. Since they started rehearsing, dinner is 'improvised', because no longer can he 'think about what to cook', like before. Improvise. I'd never want to apply that verb to things to eat. It makes me think of people who are not who we are. But since Cris we're not who we are any more.

aC, when I come home in the evening and they are re-hearsing, they don't pause and neither does the little one. The poor dog comes out. And straightaway there comes an evening (maybe the third or fourth) that I find them both, him and Cristina, preparing dinner. Salad and trout. A wholly confused 'hello,' from me. A wholly nice, musical 'hello,' from her. Two notes. Si, do? A wholly busy 'hello,' from him. Anyway, even the 'improvised' salads he makes are truly very good, unlike mine, which contain all sorts of things. He adds tomato and burrata, and if he thinks celery doesn't fit, he leaves it in the fridge even though he knows that if we don't use it soon it will go bad. I grab everything I can find. That's how we see life too, he and I. Me: everything and right now, so nothing is left over. Him: only what fits, even if what is discarded will rot.

Over dinner he's talkative, and tells us about an article he saw in the paper (he says it to the little one most of all). It's one of these curious bits of news my neighbour puts in his novels to be read as a metaphor. Two male swans have 'adopted' a plastic bottle and are incubating it, as if it were a cygnet (I did my cartoon strip about it). Cristina finds it edifying. She's pleased it's about two male swans. She talks about the wisdom of nature.

'You see? Unlike humans, who have to legislate, ask each other's permission, maintain the status quo, they have no problem doing what they want,' she says. And with that she's letting me know that because of me, my acquired bourgeois compromises, she can't skip over certain conventions that no doubt he would skip over.

I'd be proud of the reasoning if my daughter had said it. She says it and it's a bore. 'Legislate'. What a word.

He hasn't read the whole article, or seen my cartoon strip published on the newspaper's website (he doesn't look at it as much as he used to in the beginning, when of course it was a novelty). He's only read the title and subtitle. Someone must have sent it to him. If he'd read the whole thing he'd have seen at the end it said that one of the swans was dominant and the other was there by force. Maybe the dominant one couldn't find a female and scooped up the poor wretch, who never wanted to be there.

'Cristina, stay over if you don't feel like going home,' I tell her. And cough, cough, cough.

'Oh!'

No other words could have brought her more delight.

He also thinks it is a fantastic idea. He's starting to get tired of driving her. She is a copy of me, but he is his own photocopy.

So Cristina accepts. But we'd need to give her a little pot for her contact lenses. Can we? Of course, I have lots of little pots. We can. I immediately go looking for one in the cupboard where I have the new, thinner pads I bought in a pharmacy in Barcelona, far away from my usual haunts. I'm like the character in the story going to pharmacies to buy trifles like nail files, only to end up asking for the bottle of Veronal she really wanted to commit suicide.

The morning after the first night of her sleeping at home, they're all still in bed when I get back from my run at seven.

It's time to wake the little one up for school, and for him and her to go and rehearse, because they have to be in the orchestra all day today. Most importantly I'll tell them to take their scores. Most importantly, an apple for breakfast for the little one. Most importantly, most importantly, most importantly.

'Come on!' says a happy version of the Mona Lisa to her daughter. 'It's already seven, ok?'

But I have to help her get dressed.

'You comb your hair, all right?' I say. She doesn't like combing her hair and if I do it, she says I hurt her.

Cristina comes in and sits at the table. She's blinking like an adorable, sleepy Furby. She sleeps a lot. She never stops sleeping. She sleeps as much as my father.

'What would you like for breakfast?' I ask her. It'll be the first time all four of us have breakfast together.

'Anything, whatever you have,' she says.

Singular you, you, no plural now, is there? In her fantasy I suppose the domestic life to which my man is condemned is my fault, my design (she's right). This little house for the protagonists of 'No Surprises' that doesn't tally with us — better suited to a Modernist flat in Barcelona's Eixample — is my fault. It was me who wanted it, thanks to the neighbour. If it weren't for me, he wouldn't be paying half the mortgage through violin lessons and the salary from the orchestra, nor ever mash vegetables; he'd be a freelance musician and sleep in a wagon from where he'd see the stars of the gypsy night every night.

'Toast like me, cereal like the little one, nothing like Òscar?'

'Nothing?'

She still doesn't know because she hasn't slept with him or woken up with him.

'He eats later.'

'Not even a coffee?'

I'm menopausally pleased to think she'll say the words: 'Me on the other hand, — I'm not human until I've had a coffee.'

'It doesn't suit his stomach.'

And I clarify:

'It gives him the runs.'

She looks at me with pity. She understands I'm going against him with this. And it's my mistake, because she won't keep the fact that he gets the runs in mind, but that I've revealed it in order to ridicule him. But it's not true. Without her, the runs make the little one and I laugh. Only with outsiders does it become a wickedness of mine. She's the one who has altered the meaning of the runs.

'Cereal, then!' she cries.

She says it with false delight. She appears to be obliged to show interest and fascination in everything all the time. All the fascination you didn't feel when you should have in childhood. She's one of these young people who delight in biscuits, chocolate spread and cartoons. On the contrary, my daughter doesn't show interest in anything. Cristina would see a fly in flight and exclaim: 'Wow!' The little one would see a UFO land and go: 'Meh ...' Both playing a role, but they end up believing in it.

'Fine. Chocolate is the only drug we can allow ourselves now,' I say.

I say it to bring up the subject of drugs. The spider that is me has been seeking this moment for days.

'Yes.'

I'd guess she must smoke a joint from time to time but nothing else.

'That and alcohol. Goodbye to everything else,' I add.

She looks at me and nods, she doesn't know what to say. As we've said, she doesn't drink, she gets drunk straightaway.

'Everyone has a drug that they like more than any other, that they can't control. Òscar used to like Ecstasy before,' I say, 'and he always says he'd like to do it again one day, just once.'

She doesn't answer. She's listening to me. She takes me for a nutter.

'Haven't you tried it? It's a drug that makes you feel good, you feel so much love and you're especially attuned to music.'

'Really?'

This pleases her. She thinks — because all musicians do — that she doesn't play with enough feeling.

I shout for the little one again.

'Angèlica! Do you know the time?'

And the sweet voice once more.

'We must try it sometime, the three of us. On the night of Sant Jordi, when we're having the party. You will come, won't you?'

He appears. We look like a sitcom. Not even a series. Our lives aren't worthy of expert commentary on radio talk shows.

'I was saying to Cristina that one day we should try E, the three of us.'

He and I still say E, from Ecstasy's initial. Suddenly I remember the code he used to send the dealer via WhatsApp when he wanted some: 'Is Ed there?'

'Ooof ... I've lost all my contacts,' he says.

'There are ways,' I say. 'Gretchen's friends, I bet ... Not to mention Pere, of course.'

I'm referring to my first husband. I said it to observe the reaction that until now has always, always been fury when I talked about him. But he sees the little one's dishevelled head, and lets it go.

'The three of us are going to have breakfast somewhere, just in case. I'll take you to school, Angèlica, no need for you and Mama to catch the bus,' he says.

Their two faces filled with delight. They weren't comfortable having breakfast with the spider. Yes, yes. Breakfast in a bar! Everything half-finished at that table, like Pompeii. The cereal she said she wanted, the cup of milk in the microwave that had already pinged.

I wave goodbye from the beautiful, hideous, white lacquered door. I sit at the table and all alone I sip coffee with (soy) milk before I start working on a commission to illustrate a book of stories. Twelve illustrations, and I can decide what they should be. One of the stories includes a popular song called *La vella,* The Old Woman:

> *In Mallorca there's an old woman (repeat)*
> *who is a hundred and fifty-one,*
> *the buzz, buzz old woman,*
> *who is a hundred and fifty-one,*
> *the old buzzing woman.*
> *She parts her hair and combs it (repeat)*
> *Like a girl of just fifteen,*
> *the buzz, buzz old woman,*
> *Like a girl of just fifteen,*
> *the old buzzing woman.*

It seems that the old woman goes to the town square and takes a student out to dance, and promises him that if he wants her, she'll make him rich. It seems we've always existed, in one version or another.

They leave. So he'll defy the runs in a bar with good things like hot chocolate, croissants, coffees from an espresso machine with a heart drawn in the foam, that like all lefties Cristina will see upside down, like an artichoke or an ass.

While running I think:

When I grew up, I discovered that what I used to do to my uncle wasn't done with two hands but only one. I came to realise — I hadn't thought about it — that I only did it with two hands because my hands were small. 'Sexual abuse, come on, you liar,' my brother said. 'Liar, slut, luts, you like being the centre of attention, you're a slut and you always will be, you'll always destroy the people who get close to you,' he said. Was he right? Doing it was no different to changing his nappies. Would it have been considered abuse, would I have been taken to the unit if I'd only changed his nappies? For me it would have been much worse. But not worse than cleaning rabbits. Would I have been taken to the unit for cleaning rabbits? I was very lucky. I'd been brought to the unit because I'd done that. My brother was right. I liked the idea of all those psychologists making me draw pictures, far away from their brownness.

In the evening I have to go to a round table about women and illustration (it's always a round table about women and illustration). I've had it marked on the calendar for months bC, (a calendar that the little one and I draw every year and give to everyone in her class).

He has to come with me in the car, and afterwards we're going to have dinner in a three-star restaurant booked a long time ago (bC), as an anniversary present for us both. Before, he always liked to accompany me to these events that, feeling a little like an impostor, I said 'made me uncomfortable'. Not any more. Now he won't stay for the talk, he'll wait for me in a bar. Now, the things about me that please him are the things surrounding us. How I look after the little one, how we make the crib at Christmas, how I call his parents to ask how they are, the tasting menus. Not, of course, any illustrations I might make since the book of lists.

'Ask Cris if she wants to join us for dinner,' I say in a wholly natural voice, like a chatty mother pushing her shy son to invite a friend for an afternoon snack. 'I don't imagine there'll be any problem asking to add one more.'

He looks at me, without the outraged surprise that this deserves. Cristina is in the little guest room. I've said 'Cris' for the first time.

'Well ... actually today she could babysit for us,' he answers, as if reducing everything to practicality.

He means she'll also be staying over.

'We could ask your parents to stay with the little one. If it's only for her to be a babysitter, don't do it. Don't do it just for the sake of doing it. Invite her if you'd like to.'

'Like to? But you suggested it!' he answers, irritated.

'Are you annoyed?' When he gets annoyed, I always take a very bland tone, which annoys him even more.

Cristina appears, surely attracted by the quarrel and sprawls in the tableless living room. She doesn't know where to place herself, or what to do with her hands when she's not playing the violin. To me this is very cute. I try not to pay attention to his irritable tone. As if what has happened is nothing. What the little one always demands from me, when we argue. 'Let's pretend what has happened is nothing.' This is the word order, switched up and odd, not the natural 'Let's pretend nothing has happened.'

'Cristina, can you stay with Angèlica today?' he asks her, sulkily.

'Of course.'

But everything falls apart even though she immediately turns to the little one, sitting on the stairs:

'We'll have a great time today. A girls' night. A film and pizza!'

Then not looking at her, he tells her:

'You know my wife asked me if you would come for dinner with us?'

My wife. So mean in that moment.

She doesn't altogether understand. She doesn't realise I told him I was thinking of asking the restaurant with three Michelin stars to increase the reservation and be charged for another tasting menu and wine pairing (she doesn't want to know anything about tasting menus and wine pairings).

'I'd be delighted to go for dinner with you both. I like you.'

But she doesn't come. I suppose my love knows these activities are always reserved for the spouse. The older one, the one who can distinguish between foie gras and pâté.

While running I think:

As young men after the war, my grandfather and a friend decided one day that like everyone else, they too would dabble in the black market. They went to France to buy dried green beans. They saved for the ticket. They returned by train, the sack at their feet. A policeman entered the carriage and stopped them, speaking Spanish.

'What are you doing?'

'Smuggling ...' they said in a low voice.

And the policeman confiscated the sack.

My grandmother would always tell this story, cackling like a witch, as proof of my grandfather's naivety. What a downtrodden man, what a wretch, what was he thinking? But it breaks my heart to think of them planning this great exploit, 'We'll go and buy green beans and sell them, we'll bring them in by train.' Family businesses on my father's side have always been a disaster. Gabon and the Order of Malta.

I begin treating Cristina like a babysitter. Don't let her go to bed with the phone, she must do her homework, please ... But then I pull back. Better him wearing himself out.

'Òscar will explain it to you. I'm going to get dressed.'

I dress myself much more elegantly than I'd thought at first. I would have worn jeans and a t-shirt, but I put on the black dress. It's elastic. She'd fit into it, but she'd look like a sausage.

Of course she'd look like a haughty sausage and heterosexual men would look at her as a haughty, sparkling, precious sausage. I am a poor, try-hard skeleton, and just about everyone would look at me, except heterosexual men. The actress Mae West apparently said that she could tell gays at a glance because they were the only ones that didn't turn their heads when she walked into a restaurant. Women of my age and condition can say the opposite. We can identify gays because they're the only ones to turn their heads in solidarity, understanding the effort made and evaluating our outfit. The majority of heteros wouldn't do so, because they'd have no interest in taking it off us.

'You're gorgeous,' she says as I descend the stairs (always descending stairs). And instantly, instantly: 'I would definitely fall over in those shoes ... I'm such a duck.'

In that moment, in that moment when she's playing the klutz as I would have at her age, I realise she's jealous. Poor little arrogant substitute. All of a sudden I feel sorry for her. I feel sad for her, for me and for Neptune. For all the couples in the world who get in each other's way in the kitchen. For all the husbands exasperated by their wives' eccentricities, for all the wives who no longer laugh at dirty underwear thrown on the bedroom floor and wrinkled like pretzels, for all the misunderstood snoring, for my grandmother's savage laughter, for all the husbands who prefer masturbating to coitus with their spouse, for all the wives who prefer massage to orgasm.

'You two look incredible!' says the little one, referring to her father and I. 'You two'. I want to hug her for that plural.

Cristina has been flustered since sensing my intentions. I am the spider and I don't want to eat her, I want to wrap her in the larder of my frightful winter.

I utter three or four trivialities at the round table that completely take apart the title and subtitle of the talk, as is appropriate; I draw things on a little blackboard they've placed there that fascinate the audience; I pose for photos with whosoever asks me; I sign the book of lists (but nothing else), and we leave like a shot for the restaurant. I drink a lot during dinner. Champagne, Burgundy, Priorat, Montsant, port, gin and tonics. Everything. I get drunk. In these restaurants everyone gets drunk; they don't bother telling you the names of the cheeses you'll eat before dessert. You could get tofu or soap. Everyone is drunk by the cheese course.

I spend the journey home with my head against the window, coughing and fighting sleep. The little one says I snore sometimes. No one thinks that of themselves. But this time, when we're almost at our outpost, I force myself to initiate a sex act in the car. (Lubricant and I are already best friends). And he reacts, happy, jokey, surprised. No longer is it so natural or usual that I show sexual desire (and even less so in the car).

'But don't fall asleep when we get home, will you?'

Cristina opens the door for us and sees the flirty spark in our eyes. I'm doing it solely for her. If she weren't here, I'd be feeling lazy. He lets himself be loved, unaware of the shattered glass he leaves in his wake, like that 1960s cartoon character — Rompetechos, Roof Breaker, was his name — who was myopic and went around causing disasters without knowing it (I buy and sell first editions of comics on the side).

'Thanks, Cristina,' I say, between fits of coughing. Suddenly she's become less mysterious. 'Did she behave?'

'Totally! We're great friends. We even have secrets!'

She's doing it to please him. She knows there's no chance without this prerequisite. It's the little one who has to accept her, not me. Any aspiring lover who tries to be more important to a father than his daughter will lose everything.

We go upstairs. Now I must initiate the implied and promised sexual act. It has to be me. After the last time he doesn't know what to do. In the bathroom, after making the pad disappear, I look at that tube and open it. No odour, of course, just in case. But I think (and chuckle) that maybe, with such a sensitive stomach, licking it will give him diarrhoea or some intolerance, as if he'd been to an avant-garde restaurant.

We undress, without the greediness of those early years (when clothes ended up on the floor) but with the confidence of knowing — no doubts — what we have to do to each other. He gives me a sloppy yet very sincere kiss and I do let myself go and cling onto him; I want him on top of me, smothering me; wrapping my legs around his spare tyre. The palms of both his hands grab my cheeks and my lips furl as if I were a gargoyle. I want him at this moment. He pulls my hair gently, the pornographic cliché. Then I think of another old lady thing. His hands will get stuck because, oh God, since another old lady thing — thinning hair— is happening to me, I put an old lady thing on it: hairspray.

The following evening I come back from Barcelona, after drawing the comic strip at the newspaper and I find a note on the piano. 'Don't open the door downstairs.' Cough, cough. 'Downstairs' means the basement. It's because sound could flow out. He could have sent it to me on WhatsApp and been sure I'd seen it, but leaving a handwritten note on a piece of paper seems to me like a further step towards these two becoming a twosome. Like when children shut themselves up in their rooms and also write 'Keep Out', more for adults to know they're excluded from their childhood world than because they're doing anything secret. I acknowledge the note; I make no noise, walk the dog, open a bottle of bubbly (I'm up to a daily bottle since Cristina's been around, but we can't blame it all on her) and kill time before going to pick up the little one from her after-school theatre class. I've been waiting for this moment since this morning: going to pick up the little one.

But someone calls the landline, and it's not my mother-in-law, who's the only one that calls the landline. 'Hello?' It's the conductor of the orchestra: Hilari has died.

Not even in death is his first name said. Hilari is his surname. Hilari.

On the orchestra's website there's a creative photo in black and white of each musician with their instrument. For example, one of the girls looks down the length of her flute as if it were a telescope; another uses hers as a cane. These are the instructions the photographer gave them: they didn't want an overly formal website. My love has his violin under his chin and makes a funny face like a comedian in a silent film. Hilari is the only one sitting with the violin clutched in his hand, with a serious expression, without joking. He didn't want to do it at all. And now he's dead.

I go down to the basement, knock at the door, they don't hear me; I knock louder this time, they don't hear me. I have an important piece of news, them not hearing me rouses a pleasant, hybrid agitation of raw intensity in me. I call and knock. I'm eager to deliver the news. I'm eager, when they finally hear me, to see his angry face prematurely labelling me as hysterical, what does this one want now, doesn't she know she can't interrupt or the sound will come out on the recording? Turning me into what suits him.

'What!'

Such menopausal pleasure. His face. The face I've imagined is the one I see. Today he has lightly trimmed his long beard — he does that from time to time — and he smells of cologne. A hot flush comes over me. Unlike what other menopausal women say on YouTube videos, I like hot flushes. My temperature suddenly rises, my blood pressure goes down, I'm instantly sweating out of every pore. A pleasure similar to fainting. Running close to the limit, sighing, four minutes per kilometre, at the end of the course seeing the finish line — the *mirage,* they call it — there in the distance, thinking you can't do it any more.

'Òscar, Hilari has died.'

With composure. More than the 'what'.

'Oh ...' he goes.

I don't want to see any shade in his surprise, any half-sorrow, any abstract blame for an as yet unborn but present feeling for Cristina, brought on by Hilari's lung cancer; nor do I want to see a semi-happiness, an 'about time', that active, deceptive, pragmatic resignation in him I know so well, like when we play Risk and kill one of his soldiers. But then I see him bow his head. Suddenly sorrow. He feels terrible because he's criticised him. He's sobbing. My poor love, so little given to overt feelings, so mocking of sentimentality, how he sobs. How his body shakes, an unnatural way of crying, because he's not used to it like I am. As we've already said, I cry about everything.

'I made so many jokes about him,' he moans.

Rooted to the spot, Cristina hugs her violin and bows her head. The violin is like her teddy bear, like the folder you use to cover your breasts at school.

Poor thing. My poor, poor love who feels guilty. We'll have to go to the funeral and Cristina will be the official substitute. There'll be no concert this week, as a show of respect (which means even more rehearsals). But the next one, after our anniversary, yes. 'He would have wanted it this way'. Seeing them share a music-stand from the theatre stalls will be the perfect place for the cough that won't abandon me, and never again will we make the vagabonds joke now.

After a concert during the Mercè festival, Senyor Hilari complimented the jeans I was wearing and with those disproportionately large hands like creepers, mimed a gesture signalling for me to come over and he'd tell me a secret. He was Pantalone and I was Colombina (the old lady from Mallorca playing Colombina). I followed him to a corridor. Then he told me that he — he pretended he was searching for the word — a jeans fetishist. At first I thought he was exaggerating. Like people do, when someone says they are 'addicted to chocolate' meaning they like chocolate or that they 'have Alzheimer's' meaning they have a bad memory. But then he added that he looked at websites, he couldn't help it, and sometimes, when he saw pairs on the street, he'd take photos of strangers and once he'd been rebuked as a dirty old man. He knew all the brands, had opinions about whether they should be low or high-waisted, wide-legged or skinny, and would work out sizes. He thought those with prints on them were terrible. He liked this pair of mine very much. He said the word *jeans-setting* and I realised it was serious. After that secret (my love never knew it) I went to hear them play at the auditorium in Sant Cugat in a pair of grey, distressed, branded jeans, and he thanked me, lips trembling and eyes so moist it was clear this obsession dominated his days. 'These are new,' I'd tell him from time to time, when we met. And he'd always respond: 'Delicious, thank you beloved.' And he'd kiss my hand, then ask to take a photo of me. For some reason, his Versaillesian education led me to suppose he belonged to some sexual club. That he liked being a puppy for a mistress wearing only jeans and a g-string, who, once service was complete, he would pay and thank in that way. 'Beloved'.

To go to the funeral (burial, we say) I put on a new pair I bought at an outlet shop one day I was going to see him in hospital, and a black t-shirt that goes with everything, but I wonder whether to wear heels or trainers. Everyone thinks about this, the clothes for a funeral, about what they mean, and just by thinking about this, what clothes you should wear, or above all what you shouldn't, makes you feel alive, insignificant, guilty and intoxicated. Trainers, just in case. The little one will stay with Cristina. It's not appropriate for the mother of the deceased to see his replacement.

While running I think:

I really like the Catalan word *benvolguda*, which means beloved. Until now I've been a beloved woman. I like those who say or have said it to me, like Hilari. Spanish has *malquerida* — detested — but not the opposite, *bienquerida*. *Bienamada* — cherished — yes. If you type 'benvolguda' into Google Translate from Catalan to French you get 'chère', dearest, but if you write it as two words 'ben' 'volgut', you get 'bien aimée', well-loved. The same thing in German. You get 'liebes' if you type it altogether, and you get 'sehr beliebt' if you write it as two words. In Basque, 'maitea' and 'hondo maitea'. In English, however, when you type in 'benvolguda' you always get 'dear'.

We're received by a nephew. He's wearing a t-shirt from a clown festival, and I sense he's put it on to show that for him black clothing doesn't imply greater love or respect. I imagine him voting left and creating work in the neighbourhood where he lives.

'Thank you for coming,' he says. 'Especially you, Òscar.'

He doesn't know that at home, Òscar makes cruel jokes about his uncle's over-academic, rusty style of playing, that he looked down on the fact that the man never took his violin with him but left it locked in his cage at the theatre, because he didn't rehearse at home. He doesn't know that a moment ago he joked with another violinist about the things he had in his cage; a pouch of tobacco; leftover food, like cartons of stock; shoe polish; a pocket edition of *Joan of Arc* ... He doesn't know that his death has set my bourgeois, benign but desperately sad fate adrift. He doesn't know that one day

Senyor Hilari, Hilari, told me I was the wife he would have wanted. That he said it so naturally I did what my mother used to do with the slipper and said: 'Oh, come on!' and I liked it, even though it made me laugh to think I was 'the wife he would have wanted' because maybe I was imagining accompanying him to swinging nights or sado-masochistic parties with hardly a murmur. I suppose it was that. He liked me for the (false) sense of daring I radiate.

'He wrote something for you,' he tells him. 'I'll give it to you afterwards.'

'Oh really?'

A letter. Maybe jokey, maybe seeking forgiveness for the quarrels, maybe telling him for the first time he considered him a very good musician. There are people from the orchestra here and there. Everyone greets me — they think I'm the most emotional of all the partners when we go to see them and I never let them down — with a thin-lipped smile. The mother of the deceased is sprawling on a sofa in the waking room. All ready. She's painted her lips (if he or the little one died I wouldn't have wanted to even get dressed).

'Senyora Hilari,' I say. And I take her hand.

'Who is this?' she asks aggressively. 'I don't know her. Who is this, what does she want?'

My eyes fill with tears and I can't stop them. The woman's lack of tact — every social convention abandoned, except those lips she's painted, because she no longer knows how not to do it — saying she doesn't know me unleashes the flood. How strange it is to cry. It's not for Hilari; it's the liturgy, it's abstract sorrow. I'm aware I could be a mourner for hire, like the Egyptians used to have, because my main problem is that my empathy isn't well-regulated. Either none at all or too much. I would cry with equal sincerity at any funeral. I cry for me too. I make the most of it. How pitiful I am, with my jeans and lubricant. I cry because they cut my hair when my mother died, I cry for Tiet Eusebi writing the letter to the filthy woman. I cry because I won't cry for my father, I cry because my love is already replacing me, I cry for the two vagabond, for our house I had to see through Cristina's eyes to understand its utter ugliness, for my daughter, who won't have to choose like Kauffmann between music and painting, because what she has inherited is maybe and only my desire to nurture. And I also cry and laugh for poor Kauffmann, who married a bigamist. Then I cough from laughing and so on. All my body's dirty water coming out, spreading its stench, staining everything.

'One day the sun will burn itself out, right?' The little one asks me when we get home.

'Yes,' I say.

'A long time from now?'

'No ...! In three or four days.'

She laughs. She wants the upheaval of Senyor Hilari's death to pass quickly. She wants life to go on, us two on the toilet, normality. Kids do that. She's still a kid. She doesn't want to see her father like this.

While running I think:

Now I don't have periods any more, I measure time in

three-week slots. Every three weeks the white roots of my
hair are already visible and I have to dye them. But I don't
want to now. I said to him:

'I'm thinking of not dyeing my hair.'

He doesn't like it. He likes my long blonde hair.

'You'll look like a lesbian.'

'Maybe.'

'Cristina wants to move flat,' he tells me. 'Poor girl, she can't
rehearse at night because of the neighbours.'

I can only think about the moment she told him. Where?
In a bar, in the morning, drinking the coffee that will ruin
his stomach? On the phone? Did they talk about this days
ago? During breaks in rehearsals?

I show interest. More than is called for, of course. I
overdo how bad I feel that the poor girl can't rehearse at
night.

'Whatever … Tell her to come here for a while if she doesn't
find a flat. '

What would he have said if it was his mother or a friend
of mine instead of Cristina? A no, he didn't want to give up
his privacy.

'Maybe, poor girl.'

'Yes, poor girl, of course. You're working here every day
anyway.'

Wicked spider.

She moves in Friday evening. He goes to get her (and that
way help her with her suitcases and bulky things) then they'll
come get me, in the usual ugly church square.

bC he and I used to joke about the name of the square. Sant Gregori Taumaturg, St Gregory the Thaumaturge. Not Taumaturg St Gregori, with the profession first like the streets 'Taquígraf Serra' or 'Pintor Fortuny', because maybe 'Saint' in the middle doesn't seem right, but then I think it lacks a comma. Our joke is calling it 'dramaturg'. St Gregory writing for theatre. We haven't made that joke for a while. It embarrasses the marine god to make private jokes in front of her, and it especially embarrasses him that she might not understand them. She certainly wouldn't know what thaumaturge means, or have any interest in finding out, because she has her whole life ahead of her.

'Hey, thanks,' she says to me when I get into the car. Different thanks to his. He owes them to her, I accept them.

She doesn't make a move from the spousal seat, this time. No need.

'You're welcome!' I say cheerily. In a 'no bother' voice. If I show fear, she'll think I'm afraid of her.

'If you like, I'll make a lovely dinner today,' he says. He's happy.

And once on the motorway I see Cristina take out a card to pay the toll. Of course, she'll have done so all the times they've come back from rehearsals. Punctual, efficient, her ovaries functioning at top speed.

'Wow, incredible!' he says jokingly. 'She never remembers.'

He says this to the young woman, not to me. 'She' never remembers. This is the sentence that makes it official we won't grow old together, won't kiss each other's wrinkles, nor be the old people all couples in love promise each other they will. I rest my head against the window and let myself be carried away by the vibration, which reaches my teeth and elbows.

The Pythagorean cup is an invention by Pythagoras of Samos. Many souvenir shops in Greece sell them. During waterworks in Samos, in the year 530BC (Before Christ, not Cris) he regulated the consumption of wine among the workers with this cup, the 'Cup of Justice'. In the centre there is a cylinder which rises from the bottom (know what I mean, an ass?), goes down again and is connected on the other side to the inside of the cup. Following the principle of communicating vessels, if you fill the cup to a certain level, despite the hole, the wine remains within and can be drunk. But if you're greedy and fill it more than you should, it flows out and you lose it all.

'Cristina, you've not forgotten the party on Sant Jordi?' I say.

'Oh, the party ...' he murmurs.

'Oh yes,' she says.

While running I think:

Once, when I hadn't yet done the book of lists, and all my pictorial prestige remained intact, at a round table ('The Work of Female Illustrators' or 'Illustration and Women') a literary critic who had also been invited saw my mobile phone out in front. The organisers had prepared armchairs and pallets and fruit boxes that served as tables, and glasses of wine in front of us (it was interesting to see how little the speakers were drinking). All to make it welcoming.

'Do you have a kitten photo as your screensaver?' she asked me, slyly. 'I didn't imagine you like that, as a lover of kittens and such things ...'

'Such things'. She said it in an inquisitorial, sarcastic, surprised, scandalised, wide-eyed tone, 'I can't believe it, how can it be that this one, a famous lush who draws such filth, is a lover of kitten photos'?

'Ah,' I went. 'My daughter put it on there. I don't even know how to do it.'

That sentence was utter happiness. My complete happiness. No Cristina threatened me then and I was able to live 'in domestic bliss', a stranger to the outside world, not knowing how to put photos on my mobile phone. Habit, routine, the cage of marriage, all the things criticised in songs, having a dog, going to IKEA, making shopping lists — they made me want to dance. It was me who loved Christmas, me! It happened to me as it does to heavy metal musicians: after destroying hotel rooms and seeing some friend drown in their own vomit as per tradition, they have a child. And then they enrol them in a religious school, make them eat vegetables with zero food miles and ban piercings and deodorants with parabens. She saw it too. I didn't choose my screensaver; she did, she chose lots, because she hated Christmas and going to IKEA and having a dog or children, because like her profile picture, she was defined by her screensaver, but I didn't care, I didn't waste my time on screensavers or profile pictures; I'd put my daughter on there because she was what mattered. She envied me because I didn't choose my screensaver; I looked down on her because she did choose hers. Both of us conforming with social customs. She, however, was in unconscious denial. On the other hand, I was in unconscious adoration.

For dinner he makes us a salmon caviar toast (when did he buy it? Where did he keep it?) and gives it to us while we wait for the main course, all three of us sitting at the bar that separates the kitchen from the tableless living room (sitting in descending order of age). He opens the white wine for us, and grabs the appropriate glasses, the ones for white wine, and before pouring he sniffs them to see if they have a stuffy smell or dishwasher residue and as it seems they do, he then shakes them as if they were incense-smoking thuribles. He always does this, another gesture I might really miss, like the violin at his neck, like how he pulls his long parquet-coloured hair into a ponytail without looking; how he scratches his groin, which I actually like even though so many wives hate it.

Then he starts making homemade hamburgers, with buns, lettuce, cheese and good mustard. No big deal, yet it's a wonder. He always has the freezer full of food that he uses as a base to make dishes. He knows how to do things. For him, cooking is also an art. He drizzles the mustard in a zig-zag motion that would never have occurred to me. I suppose if he were to drizzle lubricant on his penis (if I dared tell him that doing so would really help me), he'd also do it like this. Zig-zags. Then he'd end up plating it up to serve me.

Cristina eats like a young person. Like me at her age, I suppose. She's one of those women who notice the candle on the table first thing (if there's no cake, because otherwise they notice the cake). If they have to cook for a lover, they'll make a green salad with nuts, organic chicken in cava and a tulip-shaped wafer cup with artisan gelato (I wouldn't dare say whether he would tolerate that now). Our daughter would do the same, if not for us concealing (the verb is exact) a love for cooking in her. I watch her eat, for the first time mundane, with everyday hunger. She must have a milky smooth body, with no muscle, and she must rapidly give in to pleasure and afterwards wrap herself in sheets that make funny baroque creases. What is surprising is that this body, so tender, so obviously cooked at a low temperature, so inactive, should belong to a violinist. To someone capable of doing what she does with a violin. To someone who's had this unnatural resolve.

We officially give her the guest room, where there is a childish little bed that no one has ever used (who would want to sleep here?) and the ironing board. The little one puts a sweet on her pillow, which she's seen in cheap hotels when her father goes on tour. Soon she'll leave clothes in the laundry basket (where will we put the laundry basket now?), at first primly (what to do with period-stained underwear?). It's not that I don't think she's pretty; it's that I find her dirty or unkempt. The misshapen, ratty shoes with tips pointing up like a clown's; buttons hanging off her coat. I would tell her to dress better. I'll end up telling her. That's what mothers-in-law do with daughters-in-law, so they may be worthy of their son. This is what … I can't say it yet.

While running I think:

Before pairing up with me, I could see all his best qualities. When he paired up with me, when he fell in love, I realised he didn't have them. Why would he pair up with me otherwise? No one of true quality could want me for me. I had that sick thought. By the following day, she already lives here and he makes us omelette with a side of endive for dinner. A homely dinner. 'Curly' endive, it's called. Four omelettes: cheese for the little one; French for me; cheese and ham for him and cheese and ham for Cristina, too (she always copies him). We drink water, but we also have a bottle of wine on the table, opened the day before. We don't uncork anything special any more. I tell the little one, 'Have some greens,' tell him to serve Cristina some greens; you have to eat your greens, it's good for your tummy, Angèlica, you know what I mean. He and the little one are happy; they can show off in front of her: they're alike in that way. He talks about music (he's already told us everything) and the little one about school. For this reason couples sometimes desperately need to go out with other couples and half-fall in love (or fall in love) with these other couples. Being able to say once more what they no longer say when they're alone. For the moment when you only say what you do, not what you think, opine, find, consider, or pleases you. Being with someone who doesn't infuriate you, being with someone who asks what you did today.

'Cristina suggested that she can contribute by being an au pair while she lives with us, picking up the little one, taking her to school, to speech therapy ...' he says, chewing a piece of omelette, in the sweet abandon of eating with his mouth full (yes, yes, I can put up with these things, I can put up with all the vulgarity of those I love, I welcome it, as long as they're still mine).

I look at the three of them. They look at me. They've already talked about it, this au pair thing. They all think it is a good idea and want to convince me. It's me who takes the little one to school in the mornings by bus (so lovely, this journey; so many stops, the same parishioners every day, the driver whose name we know ...). But now the little one will prefer Cristina taking her in her shiny new (utilitarian, small and clean) car, with an Elvis hanging from the rear-view mirror. Farewell, unilaterally happy Wednesdays, returning from extracurricular activities.

'Oh, perfect,' I say. And cough.

'This way you can draw, Mama,' the little one says. They've made her say this.

'Let's see how it goes ...' I say. And more coughing.

They look at each other. They foresaw this reaction.

Cristina clears the plates and empties them into the organic waste bucket (she already knows where it is and where sometimes she's seen half-full cans and other forbidden items end up). I can stay sitting at the table this time. He takes a bowl of yoghurt out of the fridge.

'It has grated lemon peel on top,' he announces.

'Go get bowls, Angèlica,' I say.

I'd have taken the four yoghurts out of the fridge, I'd never have thought of putting them all together and grating lemon peel on top. How does he come up with such nice things?

'Why do I always have to do everything?' the little one complains.

'Really? You have to do everything?' he scolds her.

'Come on, don't be cross ...' says Cristina.

But that was my reply. She's already stolen it from me.

The following day. One more station. She's been our au pair for a day. I arrive from the newspaper and the dog doesn't come out to greet me. That's never happened.

I realise why when I enter the living room: they (Cristina, Neptune and the little one) have let her sit on the sofa. bC it was strictly forbidden. They're watching the evening political satire programme. Three pairs of shoes on the rug on the floor.

'Can you not put your shoes in the right place?' I ask, irritated. And I add a line that I usually say with ironic intent, but it's no longer ironic because I've used it too many times. By now it's a cliché. I say: 'Must there be this travelling exhibition of shoes?'

All three laugh, not because of the phrase, but because they've talked about it. They'd predicted I'd say what I said. I always say it, but it's the first time I'm referring to three pairs of shoes and the first time three pairs of eyes look meaningfully at me. Four if we count the dog's, suddenly cured of her separation anxiety. A fit of coughing comes over me.

'Come on, don't be mad,' he says. 'And get that cough looked at ...'

'Come on, Mama ...' says the little one.

'No, she's right ...' says Cristina, like a placatory nereid.

But still a laugh escapes her. Sweat from a hot flush, a cough (which I need to get looked at). My body constantly insists on betraying me.

'I'm going to put my pyjamas on,' I say.

Yes, ok,' he says. Which means: 'Us too'. The dog gets off the sofa and then she does follow me.

All four of us appear in our pyjamas. Of course, there's a difference between these pyjamas (I no longer wear leggings). Ours: scruffy, worn out. Hers: brand new, fit for an adorable owner. Penguin pyjamas (teeny penguin pjs), well-drawn penguins it must be admitted, in the form of a onesie (which must be very warm, she wouldn't have put it on if she lived alone, if she'd lived with us for years). The little one likes it immediately ('Ohhhhhh! So cute!') and Cristina just as immediately promises she'll buy her one (if I don't mind, of course), it's from H&M. All four of us are wearing bed socks. It's not the season for bed socks, but not the season for taking them off either. We sit on the sofa, all four of us this time. He on the right end, me on the left, the little one next to me, Cristina next to him. We fit nicely. Then he grabs a reindeer blanket we have, given to us by my sister-in-law. He covers all four of us even though it's not cold.

'I'm spent,' says Gretchen when we reach the top of the mountain, which we've run up in silence except for my groans. It's already day. If we look directly at the sun rising behind the mountain we'll see little orange and pink lights afterwards.

I say the phrase we always say:

'But we're going to feel great afterwards, you'll see.'

Dani and Francina arrived at the top a minute before and are running in circles to keep warm.

'Drink water, if you feel thirsty it's already overdue,' he says as usual, because he always says this.

We drink, more to rest than anything else. Gretchen touches the marker of the mountain top.

'Come on! Touch it or it doesn't count.'

We do so, laughing in the indifferent, scientific way we do. We take a photo of us.

'All ugly except Gretchen,' complains Francina.

It's true. Her face couldn't look any healthier, she's so blonde and beautiful, 'like an influencer' (this is how we tease her), with her one breast always on show and the scar of the other we all adore and which makes her look like a priestess with prophetic powers in the Temple of Delphi. Unintentionally, because I'm sure she's never thought about it, along with that one breast all of her has become asymmetrical. She's cut her hair short on one side, but left the other side long. She wears lots of bracelets on one wrist, along with her running watch, but nothing on the other. When she runs, only one foot rolls inwards: the right one.

'The squatter is going back to live in Italy,' she tells us, as she hands the canister back to Dani. All three of us call her lover 'the squatter'.

'Oh, wow ...' I go.

'No! I was getting sick of him,' she answers. 'And my husband is suspicious.'

'You're really sick of him?' asks Dani.

It's always hard for him to stop going to bed with his ladies (all friends with lubricant, I suppose). He doesn't know how to do it.

'I could be his mother, but if I were, I'd scold him for always going around shirtless,' she laughs.

We start trotting again.

'And what about you?' she asks me. I've seemed different for days.

All three of them have this idea that mine is a happy marriage. It's not a lie. But they also know that it always depends on me. Sometimes Gretchen talks to us about her elder daughter, the one born in Germany. About how she disappoints her. 'She won't kiss me, she tells me I have a fat ass, when I was having chemo she used to say she was ashamed of me and that I stank, she writes horrible things in her diary about me.' She thinks mine loves me madly. That's not a lie, either. Her older and younger daughters will disappoint her, little by little. My only daughter will disappoint me suddenly, from one day to the next. The day before we'll have been laughing in the toilet in domestic bliss. But it's not her. It's me. I pretend to myself the ship isn't sinking until the water is lapping at my neck. And then I say: 'We're drowning! We have to jump!'

'Oh, I'm fine, I'm fine,' I say.

Since her illness Gretchen has check-ups every six months. It's always embarrassing to tell her trivial things, if we keep this in mind: she's seen death up close and every six months she has a medical examination. When she was sick she made many jokes about what runners do when a friend is gone: she asked us to make t-shirts with tear-jerking, OTT, cheesy slogans, like 'We'll always be a foursome', but it couldn't be any more true.

'Do you already have a dress for the performance?' I ask Cristina.

'No, not yet. They tell me it has to be black. I don't have any in black ... I'm more of a colour person ...'

I would say I'd lend her mine but as we've already said, she'd look like a sausage.

'Oh well, Òscar really likes black dresses,' I say as if in passing.

'Doesn't he really like trousers?' she asks.

She couldn't help it. I always wear them.

'I'm the one who likes trousers. It's all the same to him.'

'Me too.'

Me too. Of course, I think. That's why Senyor Hilari wouldn't have even looked at you.

'Do you want us to go shopping one day for clothes Òscar will like and that will work for the performance?' I ask her.

I'd never said anything so explicit. So permissive. With no comma. I've planted the 'one day' out there, to hide the perverse coalescence: pain for her, pain for me. The phrase has gone up an octave to reach the high notes. Partly because of the 'one day', like the cherry or prawn garnishing the gazpacho in modern restaurants. The necessary domesticated eccentricity. The excuse.

'Oh. Yes. You know about this kind of thing.'

She says so, but she's not sure.

'Well if you want to, the offer is there. You just name the date.'

Why did I say 'date' and not 'day'? To make it more work than leisure. 'Name the date to submit the drawing, but say what day we go for a drink'. It sounds more like an assignment you'll accept without hesitation.

'Yes, perfect, whenever you like.'

She pretends she hasn't heard 'Òscar will like' because if she had she'd have to say no. That she buys clothes for herself, not for others, all these lies. All these truths.

While running I think:

At the beginning I needed no one but him. Then I began to need the first drug, friends and a social life, because neither he nor I laughed as much when we were alone. We were no longer surprised by our respective intelligence. Everyone needs the second drug, laughter. And I already needed more than the third drug, sex, which is possible with the help of the second. The fourth, alcohol, to be able to continue having the second. Before love? There can't be love without laughter, or already in our case, laughter without alcohol. The secret of a mature, Cristina-less couple when children are already grown: wine, laughter and lube.

I send a message to my first ex. I tell him I want to see him, I'm inviting him for a drink, he has to do me a favour. He replies within five seconds, doesn't leave me 'Seen', tells me we'll go straightaway, he's delighted to see me. What has taken me so long. Cough, he's delighted to see me.

We meet at the usual cocktail bar at four in the afternoon. I order a daiquiri (sometimes I order cocktails that awaken a tropical state of being within); he, a gin and tonic. He's a fat, swollen man now (he wasn't before) but everyone finds him attractive. Like a panda, he has a black and white beard, some dark furrows around his eyes, a body covered in hair, definitely black in some parts and already white in others. He likes all women by default. If not, he's forced to pretend, and that's the only secret of his success. He likes all styles: he's a great cook who savours a beautifully simple soup made by a granny and then eats a spherified olive. He appreciates every gesture, large or small, from every woman, large or small. If one is tattooed, he appreciates that tattoo, and loudly tells everyone else about it, so we too can celebrate it. If one wears perfume, he appreciates that scent. If one has painted her lips, he appreciates that detail, because for him it's all a desire to play. An apple or a tasting menu. He likes it all. Fake breasts or real breasts, drooping or small, Gretchen's sole breast, all beautiful. His way of behaving with women is at once innocent and satyr-like. A way of behaving that trusts everything will arouse constant sensual or spicy, cryptic, flirty moments. If he fails, he laughs in surprise. If he wins, he laughs in surprise. He's one of the few men I know who still behaves like this, now everyone is so cautious in heterosexual relationships with the 'no is no' thing. 'No' need never be said to him, because he'd never ask for a 'yes' so directly. If it depended on him, by default it would be a yes from all women. From the beginning his desires float in the air, because he can't not have them; not having them would be very bad-mannered, like throwing away food. He can't miss a single opportunity. If I were to say: 'Come on, where shall we go?' he'd shout: 'Yes!' And pump his arm in a gesture of victory. Fist closed, like someone pulling the brake of a locomotive.

He's very open with me, telling me about the girlfriends he has and those who have abandoned him (we've already agreed that being abandoned is what he deserves and he takes it in good humour), because he guesses the only way he could go to bed with me again (and he'd consider it as a new notch on his bedpost, because it would be like doing it with someone else, not that Cristina I used to be) is this: talking to me about them and not pretending I'm the only one (he knows I wouldn't believe him). There's humour in him telling me the names or nicknames of his lovers. 'The Basque lasted longer than the others.' 'Sushi Chef used to say she didn't want to come to my house because they'd all left things there.' 'Wee One didn't take off her bra because she said her breasts hurt too much.' And he laughs and laughs.

'Which girlfriend do you have now?' I ask him. It's been almost a year since we've seen each other, but we talk on WhatsApp and he always likes the drawings I post on Instagram.

Laughter.

'Uf, I don't know where we were up to!'

'Me either!'

Laughter, laughter. How much I miss it, how much.

'I'm back with Xus now.'

We don't pretend to be exhaustive about it. It would be very different if he were a woman. The question would be real and the answer, too.

'Xus, who was she? I've lost track ...'

For a while he gives me a summary of Xus' life and then I tell him I need to buy Ecstasy or Molly.

'It's for me, you have to find me good stuff.'

'Is it to give meaning to your marriage?' he asks me. I don't say no. If my love knew this, he'd consider me disloyal.

He grabs his phone, which is on the bar like mine (everyone always has their phone in front of them now).

Dafne, did I leave a Beatles CD in your house?

My God, years go by and the way of doing it stays the same. Not even the musical references have changed. When we lived together and he wanted cocaine, it was the Rolling

Stones. If he wanted Molly, the Beatles. When will they stop saying CDs? I smile thinking of my man and Cristina someday, calling the dealer: 'Did I leave a Vivaldi vinyl the other day?'

Deal done. He gives me an address in a street near Santa Caterina market. We have another drink and he says he may as well come with me. We take a taxi, because he says he can't be bothered to go to the car park, take the car and find another space there. He wouldn't have done it like this if I were his wife.

Dafne's place is a drug den, tiny and dark, where every kind of drug is on the menu. I have acquaintances who live around there (they bought flats with bohemian hopes that were buried under the dirt and decay) and right now they could be recording on their mobiles to report what is happening in the neighbourhood 'faced with the district's passivity'. And they'd see me go in.

Dafne is a Brazilian trans woman who is saving to pay for the definitive operation in Thailand, she says.

'Have you slept together?' I whisper to my ex.

'She doesn't want to,' he says. And then out loud in Spanish: 'But we'll fuck sometime right Dafne?'

Dafne smiles:

'I have a very low libido because of the medication,' she replies. And as if to excuse herself, she says: 'But now I prefer a hug to a fuck.'

I burst out laughing and hug her. Massage or orgasm? Are we all the same?

The drug I want is the cheapest, but even so she gives us mate's rates. We talk about politics for a while and she tells me she has a website about transgenderism that 'I must look at'. She offers us a line of cocaine, but neither of us want it. She takes it.

When we're on the street, my ex puts his arm around my shoulders and kisses me on the lips.

'Don't go, little fool ...' he whispers. 'Do you have a curfew?'

And he licks the palm of my hand (a furtive, dry, tender, panda-like lick). What cheek, what intimacy, heart beating fast. How does he dare, I'm a lady, a lady, cheeky, what does he take me for? Should I say this to him?

He's seen something in my body language, in my eyes, my hands. When you adopt an animal, other abandoned animals appear to you. Willingly or unwillingly you give off some scent.

'I'm having a party the night of the 23rd,' I tell him. 'Sunday. I'd like you to come.'

'What will your husband say?'

Good question.

Within two or three days, Cristina is part of the family routine. If they finish rehearsals on time, he cooks dinner and she helps him. She likes helping him, because I don't like it. When I get back from the newspaper, I find the chef and sous-chef in the kitchen, her tirelessly moving the blue cloth over all the marble and the green chopping board. That blue cloth which is already hers. The way she doesn't speak betrays her. She tries intensely to enjoy the habit and she tries intensely because it's not a habit. If it were, she wouldn't be aware of it all the time. She cuts meanly, making decisions about tomatoes, watching her fingers; she can't injure them.

But on the morning of the fourth day, which is a Friday, she tells us she won't be eating dinner with us, because she's 'meeting a friend' and 'will be back late'. She's doing that thing you do when you start going out with someone. You make sure they notice you have people to have dinner with, you have an intense life outside of your love, you are someone who is loved, and you try to arouse a certain jealousy; you act as though the other person is watching. You meet someone to talk about your love and to check how much you miss them.

What does she want? Whatever she can get, for the moment. Does she want him exclusively? Certainly. We don't know much about her life. Her father is Russian; her mother, Catalan. Her sister sings. As a little girl she didn't want to be a violinist; she was very sick, she had asthma, she didn't go to school for a long time. She likes explaining this. She was given a scholarship. She exaggerates the good relationship with her exes, with whom, she gives us to understand, she goes to bed from time to time. She makes herself out to be promiscuous, but would she want to be? Or does she do it because now she should like it, because she's accidentally become a husband-stealer?

With no Cristina at home that evening, he moves from one corner to another like a soul in torment. He sits at the piano and begins to play some pieces, all in a minor key. Not a single major key, even by accident. When I hear him attack Albinoni's *Adagio* I see the situation is more serious than I thought. Then, maybe to make the sin all the greater, he moves onto the violin, and he's as sad as a musician in a restaurant or on the metro. I head up to my studio (the winter chill has reached the ground floor) after a while to avoid seeing him, who knows, sitting on the piano lid, melancholy, singing laments with a ukulele on his lap.

While running I think:

When we got angry with each other bC, the little one would come and try to get us to make up. 'Family hug!' she'd say in a deliberately childish voice, like in animated cartoons. We'd do it. Now aC, I don't scold him about anything any more. I leave underwear to wither on the floor and bottles of sparkling water with their caps missing.

'I have that thing,' I tell him. The next day is Sant Jordi.

'Oh yes?'

I see a spark in his eyes.

'Yes. It was easy, like I told you.'

'Where did you get it?'

'From Pere.'

'Oh.'

'I asked him to come to the party.'

'Oh.'

It's not jealousy, now. It's a memory of that ancient jealousy. It's rage towards me for having invited him, knowing as I do the resentment he felt for him (and that pleased me). He doesn't ask for any details of when we met up. Of how I must have been grateful to him. Me meeting with Pere remains as great a mystery as him buying salmon caviar.

'But I don't know …' He weakens. Suddenly he's afraid. 'We'd have to bring the little one to …'

'The day of Sant Jordi, if we see that …'

'I don't know.'

'Remember everything that used to happen.'

To him it seems what I want is to go back to the past, when once or twice, I took it with him (even though it had a huge effect on him and almost none on me). He thinks I want to make him feel what he used to feel for me, that sensation on the skin, the music, the kisses, that infinite love, the talking as if we were priests, so I add:

'You, me and Cristina.'

To make it clear Cristina will be there.

While running I think:

My grandmother used to drink *aigua del Carme,* a tonic for blows and shocks containing a lot of alcohol, on the slightest pretext, with any excuse. And she'd talk about her man, my grandfather: 'Your grandfather was always after me, always after me.' He was always after me. She meant sexually. She'd say it wearily, fed up, somewhat pleased, somewhat in awe. 'Your grandfather was after me until his last day. The day before he died, he was after me.' The sexual pulse of the men in my family. I wonder if it hurt her. If there was any lubricant, then.

Since the first signing on Sant Jordi is at eleven at the FNAC stand in Plaça Catalunya, I went running at seven on my own with the dog, and after showering I caught the train that brought me right there. Gretchen, Dani and Francina will come in the evening to help with the party. They'll bring food, ice and drinks. Neptune didn't want to do anything (they have to rehearse).

A lovely girl from the publisher is accompanying us as we go from stand to stand (they're divided up among the various writers). I can't remember her name, but I don't want her to know. I try to be friendly to her; I know they laugh at the authors (because they exaggerate their uselessness and oddities with covert pleasure). I greet everyone shyly (I'm an intruder) and set to work with the author of the lists, who is less inhibited and whom everyone knows. She writes a few phrases in the form of a list and I do a little drawing. Everyone comes with the book of lists; my other ones, those for children and the comic for adults, are no longer on the stand. They're the books for which I've already received the letter you get, almost always in the summer, to inform you about the 'special operations' they're doing on one of your titles. Special operations means they're being pulped because they're taking up space in the warehouse. I wouldn't be at all surprised if my neighbour used that as a title for a novel.

I'm wearing contact lenses to be able to see people and the street names from afar, but this means I don't see up close and I make ugly strokes with my pen. I could put on my glasses to write, but 'there's a cougar on Mallorca street' ... Cough.

The city centre is crammed with people: you can't walk up the Rambla de Catalunya or the Rambla de les Flors, or the cross-streets. Everyone's going up and down with books and roses. There are improvised rose stalls (trestle tables swathed in Catalan flags) but some with second-hand books too. Queues and queues forking towards different authors, with security guards letting people through when it's their turn. They ask for a signature, but also for a selfie. During the breaks, journalists ask writers how the day is going, and they say very well, it's very exciting, but they can't hang about answering questions for too long because they must sign, since it's the 'readers' day'. Most of their statements won't be broadcast, because they're all copies of each other and copied from previous years. They also question me and the writer of lists. They question everyone and perhaps that night they'll broadcast the words of those who sell the most.

In my bag I stash presents and roses and even now, the number or email of some young artist or some young writer. Of course, there are those who've come to seduce us (if they succeed, it would be something funny to tell their friends between laughs: 'Guys, guys … !') I find them all very skinny with very tight trousers. Their appearance is a mixture of takeaway delivery boy and stand-up comic. The way to be a young man or woman has changed while I was off the market on mental maternal leave. Anyway, these boys aren't choosy. They write to all the authors and only those unaccustomed to receiving letters feel singled out. I know one of these boys has slept with three of the bestselling authors of fiction as well as the co-author of the second bestselling non-fiction. He has a culture podcast and if you don't answer his emails or re-post him, he gets angry and threatens to destroy you with a review. When a new author or artist appears, he writes to them, even if they've done a book about green juices or lists, like me.

Fed up, one day I invited him to dinner and he talked about his mother a lot (they lived together and had a great relationship, he stressed). All the while he was telling me that she admired me, would be delighted to meet me, if I did a drawing for her she would frame it, yes on a napkin, please. He was sending her messages all through dinner and it somehow seemed to me that from a distance the woman was offering me her son. The boy drank very little, he did nothing but say again and again that he liked Monastrell wine, and ended up boring me. It's better never to meet this kind of very honest and touchy person, because the day always comes that without knowing why, they're vividly, delicately and persistently offended by you, and the rancour will endure for years.

At one I see all the missed calls from Neptune. I dial his number (he's one of my favourites).

'Finally!' he says, exasperated.

Bad mood, introspection. He'd never use that tone with anyone except his mother and me.

'I've barely stopped,' I exclaim. 'What is it?'

A professional 'what is it', too. Like being at work.

'Where are you having lunch?'

'Buffet at the publisher's. No remedy for it.'

I always end up adding my name to sentences.

I use the marital tone I always do. I don't use the happy, excited tone Cristina would on hearing his voice, the tone a Sant Jordi in Barcelona deserves. Not that he asks me how it's going, whether I've done a lot of signing or not. Comparisons. He's definitely rung her too. He definitely wasn't happier — he's not happy any more, never will be again — but definitely more tender, more interested in listening, more upset by possible silences. He and I are like the President of America and the President of Russia on the phone.

The publisher has a standing lunch for its authors on the terrace of a hotel on Passeig de Gràcia (everyone has to go and sign in the afternoon). There are all sorts of canapés I'd happily draw (cherry tomatoes and burrata on long skewers, black plastic spoons with salmon sashimi and hamburger sliders). I don't feel like going because I don't like fighting for food and I don't know any of the authors or the managers and directors of the publishing house.

Him:

'The little one and I are coming to see you this afternoon. I've left her with my parents for now.'

Me:

'Yes, she's having lunch there. Don't come now, it's rammed with people and very hot.'

Him:

'We'll see, maybe I'll feel like it later.'

All the publishers complain that a Sant Jordi falling on a weekend (like this year) is worse than a weekday, because if it's a weekday people leave work and browse books on the street, but if it's a weekend, many don't come.

While running I think:

'I'm the last violin in the second row,' he told me when he gave me a disc on which he'd participated, the day after meeting each other. 'You'll make me out of all twenty-four straightaway.' And I asked him for a date. I think a lot about the light of those days.

We sign, sign, sign. I look at the readers and try to work out whether they have sex. Most of our queue doesn't, it seems to me. How did Mrs Robinson do it? Had she already applied lube when she appeared before the boy?

'Women are the ones who take the initiative, the ones who really decide,' men say (Dani first, Pere second) to make us happy. After a certain age, it can't be any other way. Cats advertise being in heat: I'm available. Humans, too. You can't say, there in the parked car at the viewpoint with Barcelona at your feet: 'Hang on a minute, back in a sec, I'm going behind that tree to apply my friend. Wait while I put away my glasses. Have you already taken the Viagra? Remember, don't grab my hair. How long before it takes effect? We can chat in the meantime if you like, but then I'll have to re-apply the lube.'

Another stop, this time on the Rambla Catalunya.

'What do you want to drink?' the bookseller in charge asks me.

'Could it be a gin and tonic?'

They laugh. At first they don't know whether I'm being serious or not. They mean coffee or sandwiches. Each person has a cut-off time before which they have never or would never drink a gin and tonic. Ten in the morning. Seven in the evening. Four in the afternoon. Twelve midday. And along we come, we drunks of different degrees.

'Hey!' a short man inside the stand says to me.

My mind is blank for three or four seconds. The short man is my second ex Jordi, the graphic artist, graphic artist Jordi. The graphic novel author for whom I worked as a colourist. How could I not recognise him?

'Hello, I didn't recognise you!'

I always say this, but no one believes me. They think I'm being funny or don't want to say hello. 'So stupid,' they must think. 'So myopic,' they should think.

I look at him up close. Like a cousin, I give him two pecks. 'Where are you having lunch?' I ask him.

He doesn't have a queue of readers, but we do. Readers are more interested in lists to improve your life than illustrated dystopias about zombies during Nazism, even though I'd done the background.

'Me? At home. I'm not invited to any publisher lunch. I'm no one now, I'm not a celebrity. My publisher can't even stump up for peanuts. I'll have to illustrate a book of lists or something like that ...'

His main characteristic, which ended up driving me crazy, is that he's incapable of sounding ironic.

Ten completely forgotten years with him. What colour were the sheets or the bedspread we had? Did my then mother-in-law, who loved me so much (she's dead now), give them to us, and were they the ones with an amoeba pattern? Or had we bought them ourselves when we still had sexual chemistry and therefore it was all one colour, purple or black, suitable for dedicated sex? Did we have a bolster pillow or two individual ones? How can I not remember all those ten years but recall those in the unit perfectly? We mustn't have had a bolster pillow, they're uncomfortable, even when you love each other. We loved each other very much in the early years (later on, I didn't any more). I do remember the breakfast mug (yellow, IKEA). I've not had so much, so often, so peaceful a breakfast with anyone else.

How old he looks. Old in the way that lean people become old, like a faun. Now he's thin and he has flabby jowls from losing weight, as if he were a Muppet. How must he see me? I guess from the things he draws that he still likes women.

Men perhaps never stop feeling attraction, as my love told me that day. Many women don't either, of course. Perhaps the only one who feels nothing, nothing, nothing, nothing, nothing, nothing, nothing, nothing, nothing, nothing, nothing now is me. Nothing nothing nothing nothing nothing nothing. Is that true?

I say to my ex:

'Hey, I'll stand you a drink. I'll skip the publisher lunch. Come on, you want one?'

And he does exactly what he used to when we were together:

'If I don't put a little something in my stomach ...'

When we were together, I always thought he talked like an old man. Now he finally is an old man. Now he's arrived at the age he's always been since the age of thirteen. He feels comfortable where he is.

'Some fries maybe? I ask him.

And like before, as always, he specifies:

'Chips? Fantastic.'

Chips, of course; it's more authentic. He likes to eat very simply. He likes charcuterie (ham, sausage), croquettes, tomato-rubbed bread, potato omelette, ice cream, cakes ... He's one of those who laughs at nouvelle cuisine, makes jokes about spherification (I like it all). He spends his life on a diet.

He tells me:

'You look good.'

Me:

'Look at you!'

A joke so he doesn't get carried away. 'You look good' isn't the same as 'You're looking great ... .' It's like vegetables being good. Good, yes, as vegetables go. You wouldn't say that about a prawn. We recognise the merit of a vegetable. We admire a prawn.

There's a moment in life when every time you're near someone you've slept with you feel uncomfortable. You don't look him up and down. You don't want to touch him, that someone, in case the electricity (on his side) is still there. You don't want him to touch you, in case others see that old intent and because you'd have to reject him — rejecting embarrasses you and makes you feel bad — so you pull back gracefully like the tentacle of a snail, because you don't want him 'to be confused'. But after the soy milk another era is ushered in when this is no longer the case. You see someone you've slept with and it's as though nothing ever happened. I'm not the person who slept with him, the one who lived under the same roof as him and slept under those sheets I can't recall. I'm not her.

We come to the end of the queue and I drag him to the cocktail bar (telling him once more not to worry, it's on me) because some lemony cocktail would go down very well and because I don't want to waste time arguing in the sun — we have little time before the afternoon signings. You have little time? Then drink fast.

The difference between him and I is that for him being an illustrator (not illustrating, being an illustrator) is the most important thing. Not to me. Running is more important to me. Pets. Alcohol. Music. Family. Everything I am to lose.

He says what everyone says to me:

'You're everywhere, aren't you?'

He means he sees my cartoon strip and he's seen the poster I designed advertising a bank's mortgages (of course he would never 'sell out' like that). It's a deliberately childish house, as if a kid had done it. It's what they wanted.

I answer as I always answer, too:

'Like a slave.'

We go into the cocktail bar. In these menopausal circumstances, the blast of cold air is the only stimulus capable of raising my nipples.

'I'm here with a friend, he's an illustrator too,' I remark to the bartender (so if he doesn't recognise him, he won't be offended).

And as he usually does, my ex gives him his hand and says:

'Jordi Larreula.'

He always feels obliged to give his full name. He's had cards made, but he holds onto them if he thinks his fellow conversationalist doesn't deserve one, pretending he's mislaid them:

'I don't have a card on me right now ...'

We sit at the bar (even though he doesn't like counters, preferring a table and chair, because he's always complaining about back pain). Still the same as before, with a dark goatee and smooth hair like a musketeer, still like an Egyptian figure we saw together at the Louvre called 'The Butler Kety'. I don't know if studying Fine Arts has made me see sculptural or pictorial resemblances in everyone, or maybe it was because I kept seeing them that I studied it. That character was a marital joke. That I do remember. But not the sheets.

'So Carme is well?' And I cough.

'Carla.'

The gnome didn't get it wrong on purpose.

'Ah, I meant Carla!'

'We're not together any more, you remember that, I told you.'

I don't remember that either. How did he tell me? On the phone? I remember when he ceremoniously summoned me to 'let me know' he had a partner. He did it to maintain a pretence in front of her. He must have told her I still loved him to raise his worth. I don't lose any sleep over whether he has a partner or not. I prefer him to have one, so he'll really be happy.

'Oh no.'

He tells me he has a girlfriend now (young like the previous one) and they do the 'living apart together' thing and surely I must know her (he takes an evil pause), Marta Saperas (I do know her, she was the one who saw my kitten screensaver; who reviewed an illustrated book of mine about puberty in Time Out some time later, a grouchy, condescending review).

'Yes, I do know her.' With a smile greater than him, her and fine art in general.

While running I think:

The day I went to the health centre about the cough, I read the advice on the screen while I waited. 'Do you often get lost?' 'Has this always happened to you?' 'Is your child very fidgety?' 'Do you think they might have ADHD?' Yes, no, no, yes.

To distract myself, I do the entire alcoholism one. I remember it from top to bottom, which is a trait I have in common with the little one. We can remember all sorts of things that take up headspace yet we can't remember what we truly need to, like my second ex's girlfriend's name, who we could nickname Lady Butler Kety, or the homework for tomorrow.

'Do you think drinking alcohol influences your decisions?'

Yes, I thought. If I drink, I decide to drink more and eat processed foods like fries (I mean, chips).

'Do you practise risky behaviours when you drink alcohol?'

I don't know. I argue. I shout. I become aggressive.

'Have you ever tried to stop drinking for a week or longer, without being able to last for that long?'

I do so once or twice a year, already suffering on the first day.

'Are you annoyed by other people trying to persuade you to give up drinking?'

They've not done that. I suppose it would annoy me.

'Have you switched from one kind of drink to another to avoid getting drunk?'

Not for that reason.

'Have you had to drink first thing in the morning over the past year?'

Yes. Always.

'Do you envy people who can drink without getting into trouble?'

I am one.

'Have you had any problems related to drinking over the past year?'

Yes. It's a long story.

'Has your way of drinking caused problems at home?'

No. bC he would be doing the same.

'Do you try to get extra drinks at parties for fear of not having enough?'

I don't go to parties where such a fear could exist. If necessary, I bring them.

'Despite there being occasions on which you can't control yourself, do you continue saying you can stop drinking whenever you like?'

I think I can. But I don't like the idea. ('Oh Lord, give me chastity, but do not give it yet,' said St Augustine).

'Have you missed work, university or school because of drinking in the last year?'

No. But I've gone there drunk or merry and the following day regretted it and worried that they'd noticed.

'Have you ever had 'blackouts' (forgetting your actions) because of drinking?'

Yes.

The questions seemed unsubtle to me, made for someone who wouldn't recognise water in a line-up. They were missing: 'Since the menopause do you get drunk faster than before with a lot less than before?'

But it said if you answer 'Yes' to more than four questions you're an alcoholic.

Then, leaving the cocktail bar with my second ex, I see them. It's him, my love, the father of my child, the one who deposited semen inside me, strolling with the reboot of me. They're clearly strolling in the direction of the cocktail bar, which was mine, became ours and will be declared as 'a neutral zone' now. He's walking slowly by her side, unlike when he's on the street with me and the little one. He always walks ahead at top speed with me and the little one (we always joke about it).

'Oh look, Òscar and a colleague from the orchestra,' I say to my second ex in a casual voice.

They're having a good time talking and now they'll have a good time drinking (this time she will drink, let herself be advised, shyly; he loves giving advice). Nothing more for the moment. They're not touching (not that they'd have dared on a day like Sant Jordi, where everyone is on the streets and you meet everyone), but certainly as a joke she'll put her hand on his back to brush away a speck of dust; he'll touch her nose as he would a child's, when you pretend to have taken it (it was something he used to do to me and the blend of adulthood and childhood would bring tears to my eyes). They're not lovers, not yet. They're in the prelude of falling in love. Admiring one another. I admire you. The responsibility is mine, the sorrow too. I like you. The responsibility is yours, there'll be no sorrow.

She's carrying a rose. But he mightn't have given it to her. Or he might have given it to her to no purpose (he didn't give me roses at the beginning and that was funny; he only does so now, because it's expected, and all that's expected). He thinks I'm at the publisher lunch. He's certainly going to our cocktail bar with her because of that. No problem with the fact the bartender will see them. He's seen me just now with my ex, too. We're modern and love one another; so he meets up with women, I meet up with men. I do all my interviews in this cocktail bar. So does he when he plays in jazz quartets (so all the photos of all our reviews in the newspapers, etc, are at that bar counter). Now, very lightly, he puts his hand on her shoulder. The gesture courteous people make when they give way to you at a door. He isn't holding onto her, merely accompanying her. But the gesture affects me in a way I'd not thought it could. I could fall to the ground, like the day I read that word in the dictionary. I imagine the drawing: a woman, with her right hand on her chest, and the other behind her leaning against a wall. Her flagging legs and an expression of fright on her face. And in the background (done by the colourist), people coming and going who don't see her.

Nevertheless I prepare to enjoy his surprise and guilt when he sees me (hot flush). Like a placid, worried bumblebee, I hope I can uncover the reaction in order to study it. I have time to think about mine. What should it be? Spontaneity, confusion? Cynicism only he can see?

Him: surprise, shame, a touch of guilt and antagonism. He didn't like me.

'Hey, weren't you going to the publisher lunch?' he says to me.

Me: cynicism, morbidness, masochism, exaggeration, drama.

'I was, but I met Jordi. You? Weren't you going for a walk with the little one?'

'Yes, but Cris was coming in too and we said ...'

Cris, Cris, Cris ...

What should we do, or not do? All four of us (suggested by me) go into the cocktail bar. All four of us at the bar. My love and I in the middle. Her on his side. My ex on mine. Neither he nor I choose it, but Cristina and my ex (for some unknown reason it's really hard for me to call him Jordi) do. I've slept with both of them; she hasn't slept with either of them yet.

I shrug off laziness and start on the painful road of feminine complicity. To do so I knock back a Sidecar and a margarita at top speed.

'Easy, you know that ...' he says.

'I'm going easy.'

Then I have to go. The fans of lists await me at four.

'We're having a party tonight,' I say to my ex, because I'd neglected to tell him. 'I'd like you to come. Cristina will be there.'

'Oh all right then. I don't have anything better to do,' he says.

In another time my love and I would have looked at each other.

'Can I bring someone?'

'No way!' I joke.

All three stay put (my ex isn't signing in the afternoon). Then maybe it will be just the two of them, alone at last. Who will pay? Not Cristina; she's too young. Thanks to the soy milk, like a clairvoyant I see the scene that must unfold: my ex slowly, heavily, takes out his wallet and puts ten euro on the tray. Then he sees that ten euros isn't enough to pay for the single cocktail he's drunk and rummages to find the missing two euros. When he sees me leave he starts to worry the bill will be split. He's banked on not having a second cocktail in case the bill wasn't shared, but (at the same time) if it is shared it's worth ordering another, because otherwise he'll be losing out. In the end my man (who's a man of the world) tells him no need, no need, he'll pay. The other instantly accepts. Cristina thanks him. However, my man will send me an admonishing message later, telling me what 'the joke' cost him.

I drink for the rest of the afternoon. I've started and now I can't stop. I reach the stand I need to and say, one moment, I'm going to the toilet. I go into a bar full of people, and manage to get the waiter who recognises me (even though he doesn't know my name) to fix me a vodka and tonic before everyone else in the queue. I go through the day with very little coughing. No need to change, then.

It's not warm that night. I vividly recall the temperature of every Sant Jordi of my life as an artist, because I vividly recall what I was wearing.

When I was younger, I worried I'd be cold, because I enjoyed wearing transparent clothes or light, ripped t-shirts. An illustrator can do that. For my first Sant Jordi in 2000, with a book for five-year-olds about washing your hands, I wore a short blue skirt all day and I put on a long black one for the publisher's party that night. They were cheap clothes. I was a Cristina then and didn't realise. I simply didn't see them, women like I am now. I've just remembered, because I'd completely forgotten, that I went to bed with a grey-haired Galician poet, who I pretended to have read.

In the evening, our ugly little strip of garden with artificial grass is full of people. Some musicians from the orchestra; our neighbours (the writer and his wife); two boys from the Politics section of the newspaper where I draw; Gretchen with her Viking and daughters; Dani on his own; Francina with her wife and daughter. We drink wine, eat tomato-rubbed bread with charcuterie and Gretchen's hummus. I ordered potato omelettes from a cook at the school, as if everything were normal, as if we might continue being these leftwing, progressive yet ironic people (we're capable of making politically incorrect jokes about the climate) who buy potato omelettes from the cook at my little one's school, whose omelettes are so good. 'Look me up on Facebook,' the fat woman in white Crocs always tells me. She always says she has all sorts of famous clients she can't reveal. In the ugly garden I explain this while everyone is eating them and discovers that yes, they are indeed very good, the woman is a master of potato omelettes, words to that effect, when nothing is worrying you. And inside I'm saying: 'It's today, it's today.' Unable to think about any other catastrophe: not hurricanes, or pain, or hunger, or Senyor Hilari.

Where is he? Where has he been? We have to be seen together for a moment to make a toast in front of everyone, because it's our anniversary party. But I can't find him. My second ex and his girlfriend, Marta Saperas the reviewer, are sitting on the plastic garden chairs, watching us with their perpetual irony. How I would have despised them if it hadn't been for the circumstances of the cough. She's the youngest and ugliest person at the party (my writer neighbour's wife is second): she has a soft, saggy ass and is renowned for her late night bar-hopping, trying to get any drunk person of any sex into bed. They'll enjoy criticising me when they're alone together because I've sold so many books of lists (and will be on the list of bestsellers), but they don't know I'm a poor old woman.

She's the hipster, the one who has to look at us with sardonic condescension and overdone surprise. He's the introvert. The kind of artist who'd have excelled in a past era, in which only those who knew how to paint would dare, and his hipster girlfriend would have been a coarse, shameless innkeeper, serving pitchers of wine in the background of the painting.

They watch us, but above all they try to make it very obvious that they're trying to hide the fact that they're watching us. I should ask him what sheets we used to have.

Perched on the windowsill overlooking the garden, I start to dance. I dance and dance because I've been drinking. It's modern music, the kind I like. Bowie, the Beatles ... My love ignores it, because he thinks it is too simple.

Gretchen gets up to dance with me. From inside, the light on the piano projects our shadows on the bamboo — so invasive — plant. She moves like a stripper, showing off the shape of her breast to everyone and caressing her asymmetric hair, even blonder since chemotherapy. I playfully copy her movements. I'm a good dancer, everyone says so, but nothing compared to her. Then Dani and Francina come, and from under the window they motion like worshipping priests at us. He kneels and throws his body backwards as if he were an acrobat. More shy, she moves her hands like an Egyptian and out of the corner of her eye looks to see whether her wife is disapproving or laughing. My writer neighbour does laugh, looking around at the other guests, wanting them to participate in this unique phenomenon he finds so amusing. It's a while since my first ex left with a mum from school, who came without her husband. Poor man.

Then Cristina changes the music. She puts on the *Requiem in D minor*. She actually did it. She went to the speaker (a speaker Dani brought from the gym classes), grabbed my Neptune's phone, connected it and put on the *Requiem in D minor*. So she knows the password. Or maybe it doesn't have one (I don't know whether it has or doesn't have a password). Or maybe she's asked him for it. Taken aback (taken aback by the concert), Gretchen, Francina and Dani stop for a moment. But I keep dancing and then so do they, as if it were pop music, and those from the orchestra clap. It's like one of those CDs from the 80s ('Hooked on Classics', they were called) in which classical pieces were set to electronic drums and clapping hands. And the four of us make slow but coordinated movements, like aerobics, and we look like four hippies merging with the cosmos.

While running I think:

'Has anyone's pee been red?' I asked at home less than a month ago, bC. 'Yes!' said the little one. Me: 'It's because of beetroot, beetroot makes your pee red. It'll happen to your poo too, keep that in mind!' Because I'd made them beetroot juice. Both being so neurotic, I didn't want them to think that they had some ugly disease.

Gretchen and Dani hug me. Francina gives me a playful slap on the head. He asks me:

'Girl, why are you crying?'

'I'm so drunk.'

'It's definitely more than that.' Gretchen says.

'I wet myself. I piss myself a lot.'

We burst out laughing. And then after laughing the cough and after the cough, everything that follows. I climb the stairs to the upstairs bathroom, mine and the little one's, that is so small.

'Come on, nitwits,' says Gretchen.

And I laugh even more, because she always makes me laugh when such innocent insults no native would ever say slip out in that Teutonic accent. Nitwits. Snot comes out of my nose from laughter. Spilling is the thing. I am the Pythagorean cup. I spill if I'm overfilled. I've just realised.

They follow me. I'm so drunk I don't care if they see — or maybe I need them to see — the incontinence pad. They lock the door and sit in a heap on the floor. Everyone will think we're doing drugs. There are drugs, another father from school brought them. I have the ones from Dafne too, but they're for later.

'I piss myself too, everyone,' says Francina.

And she merrily takes out a pad to show us, as if it's a fillet of hake.

'Don't worry,' says Dani. 'There's no danger at this age: you hardly ever laugh. I speak from experience. Around seventy you'll get the laughter back'.

'I'm pissing myself!' shrieks Francina, and clutches her stomach.

'You'll stop pissing yourself when you stop coughing, idiot,' mumbles Gretchen, who's laughing too. 'And you'll stop coughing now, because it's a nervous cough. You've hardly coughed today.'

I look at her as if she's given me a divine revelation.

'You're right. It's because I'm laughing right now!' I shriek too.

'It's not the same as when you cough!' says Francina, wiping away tears. 'The ha, ha, ha must be avoided!'

Apocalypse means 'revelation'. There are revelations that appear in moments of ecstasy. The body continues on Earth, but communication is maintained through the spirit. Are we in a moment of ecstasy? Maybe so. She's said I won't cough anymore.

'And by the way, nitwits, I'm back in chemo.'

Cristina walks on tiptoe; she's an elegant and mysterious cat. What does 'elegant and mysterious' mean? Slow. But she's also explicit like they are. She displays her ass like cats do, as if she had a tail. A tail swishing slowly, flicking here, flicking there. I can see it, this tail. So can the guests. My perception has been mistaken. I see her as soft, but all the men at the party see her womanly body, womanly skin, womanly shape, womanly breasts. Neptune and nereid.

I go upstairs to put the little one and her two friends sleeping over to bed. I find them rummaging through my wardrobe, putting on dresses and shoes. I like that they like my clothes. I tell them to turn off the light, the guests are leaving. Not looking at me, speaking very, very fast, my daughter says:

'YesMamayeswe'llturnitoffnow!'

'Don't make me say it again.'

I'm so sleepy because of the bubbly that I lie down on the bunk bed and from there I look at them, laughing, excited, on the inflatable bed they like so much.

'Ah, I'm falling asleep,' I say.

They don't know I'm drunk. They all like me being there, succumbing, and so does my daughter, because the others, seeing me as a crazy mother, make the sweetness she doesn't know she has for me flow out.

'Don't snore, Mama.'

While running I think:

I've loved her since she was born like someone sliding through jelly, with no effort and in the idealised, immature, certainly hysterical and obsessive way I do everything. I knew immediately why it was that way. The love for her was the only one that didn't subside in time. Routine didn't kill it, that love. On the contrary. All the routine was for that love. A partner might end up causing disgust, pain, fear, rage, loathing. A child too, but you've no choice, you keep on loving them. Love, love, crazy love, bulletproof, that love. Then you read in the weekend supplements that it's about 'not feeling guilty if you weren't as happy at the arrival of a child as you were expected to be.' I was, completely. So much so saying it was uncomfortable. Gretchen too. Gretchen says her natural state would be being constantly pregnant. She says she likes being pregnant more than anything else in the world and if it hadn't been for cancer, she would have had more and more children and worked as a surrogate.

When I go down, I feel renewed. Maybe an hour has gone by. Now I'm able to continue drinking with no cough. I move towards the party. A divorced father is sleeping on the sofa and another is taking photos of him on his mobile, laughing. People are making a move (this is how it's said, you're told like this: 'We're making a move'). The town gardener, who makes a lot of money because he looks after the gardens of all the houses, wealthy or otherwise, is snorting cocaine.

'Come on, we're going to bed,' I say.

'Throwing us out already?' he says. For him, the party is only getting started.

I hug Gretchen, Dani and Francina.

'You're gorgeous in civilian clothes,' I tell them. It's true. I'm too used to seeing them in black leggings and race t-shirts.

'We'll go out tomorrow if we wake up in time,' he says. 'We need to purge our sins.'

'Yes,' I say.

We kiss one another and we say goodbye.

While running I think:

I always tell the little one time goes by more slowly for her than for me. When I was little I couldn't wait for the Three Wise Men to come with presents for Christmas either. All mothers say so. Before summer used to be so long, now it passes in a breath. I tell her that maybe the dog, whose life is much shorter, sees time pass in an even more intense way. Because of this she doesn't remember the things that happened a moment ago. It's the body's defence. Maybe the same thing is happening to me.

My love, Cristina and I are left alone.

'Let's have one last drink,' I tell him. 'I've not seen you all night. Where were you?'

'That was you! I've not moved from here. You disappeared.'

I go to the toilet to put on lubricant. It's true that I haven't coughed any more.

'Shall I make you both something?' he asks me when I come back to the stone bench. This 'you both' makes all my feelings abandon me.

'Yes,' she says.

'I'm hungry now,' I say. And grab chips off a cardboard tray out there.

'Don't eat that!' he scolds me.

He doesn't like salty snacks. He says they stink. I'm the opposite, I want salt on everything.

'Also, if you eat, *it* won't make us as high. Do you still have it?'

Cristina takes a chip. Suddenly chips are dignified.

'How can you?' he says. And laughs. It puts us on the same footing.

'Yes, I have it,' I say.

'I'll pass,' says Cristina.

He goes to the kitchen and makes us a cocktail (I hear the clink of the ice in the cocktail shaker: a sound that's also part of us). He puts two glasses on the plastic table in the minuscule strip of garden and fills them. They're not for him and me. They're for Cristina and me. At first, the liquid looks white but it's turning green. We taste it, we find it good, we drink.

'I do want some, if you have it,' he says.

I go to the spice rack in the kitchen and take out a little plastic bag.

He instantly remembers what he has to do. He wraps it in

cigarette paper as if it's a firework and swallows it.

'What about you?' he asks me.

I go to the fridge in search of a bottle of bubbly. Just for me, they don't want any. I uncork it and with the upper part of my thumbnail I smooth out the silver foil of the tip until it's flat. I make it into a square. Then I make a little box out of it.

I don't know. Maybe later.'

I put on music. My kind of music.

'This always gets me going,' I say.

I open my arms. I touch the back of his neck, and her neck.

'Sure you don't want any, Cristina?' he repeats.

But she doesn't answer. Better that way. She could still accuse me of 'chemical subjugation'.

'Come give me a hug!' I say then. I say it in such a way that if they don't want to, I seem drunk.

Puzzled, he laughs. He's getting high.

I give him a kiss on the mouth while continuing to embrace her. I grab the back of his neck so our heads touch. I could still pass lice to them; the little one had them a few days ago and I still have to do 'the head check' on her. When she has them, so do I. Baffled lice on that pink head.

'I love you both,' I lie, because I don't love her. Only him. I give her a kiss on the cheek and him on the mouth.

'Do you both love me?'

'Yes,' he says. 'So much. I love you so much, more than life itself.'

The drug is taking effect. Like it used to. Those amorous eyes of Neptune's.

Now it's Cristina's turn. She can say we're drunk, it will

be fine. She can say she's going to bed, it will be fine. She can give me a kiss, for a start. That will be the permission to give him one.

I stroke her pink hair. I take a lock and curl it around my fingers, as if I want to make a corkscrew out of it. I give her a kiss. Then I grab his head. All three of us kiss. Noses, somewhere in the middle.

'Yes ...' he says weakly.

I walk backwards with them to the artificial grass. I take their hands and oblige them to take each other's. I have an amorphous sexual desire. I pretend I'm drunk and reckless, I don't know what I'm doing, I won't remember it, I'm not thinking of the girls upstairs. I take off my clothes. It's too cold to go to the communal pool (and the writer's wife would see us). I help them undress. Being a man or woman doesn't matter any more. We do what we can. He is the soloist, I'm the one turning the page; he's been the quickest to adapt and is trying not to neglect us now. If it's my turn below, it's hers above. He laughs, surprised. Because of the luck he's having or the misfortune? Any friend of his would say luck. Not because of us two, but the concept we embody. We're a threesome. Dani asked his ex for a threesome as a birthday present. She didn't take it very well. I feel embarrassed about touching her and have no interest in her pleasure. He's another thing altogether. I know his body, I know what he likes as no one ever will; I've worked it out, he'd never have confessed it to me, he wouldn't have been able to. Do I make Cristina lick him in the places I know? Would I like that? It's he who wants Cristina to lick me. He owes it to me. They owe it to me. I feel like a theatre director I saw once, on the stage directing the actors while they performed before the audience. Soon we'll do what we have to do. He wants to penetrate me, he does so, and I ask him to go slow: it has to be that way with me, now. It's more reluctant porn than love-making. Threesomes aren't for me. I'm too self-centred, I don't want to share, but now I have no choice (a fad for a triad). Then it's her turn. He can go fast with her, so much lubrication, what excessive lubrication, squelch-squelch, young people. Finally, it's his turn, and tenderly he warns us he's about to come.

I'm much smaller than him. This makes me feel like a teaspoon with a soup spoon. Like a finch in a hand. Like the little one on my shoulder. Being a small woman makes everyone embrace you and makes you the embraced one. This makes you feel like a child your whole life, whether you like it or not.

The dog comes down the stairs and looks at us. He, Neptune, instantly falls asleep there; not a second has passed and he's already sleeping, already snoring. Cristina and I laugh. I cover him with the blanket my sister-in-law gave us and leave (I don't want to know what she does). Other men have been interludes, corks, bandages. He's the one and only. I love him and the desire I've had for him to love me came not from my chest but my hips. It's just that suddenly, from one day to the next, I grew up to be the exact age I should be. If Cristina hadn't appeared, I could have been *faking* for a few more years.

The following day, when my watch alarm goes off, I realise I haven't coughed all night. I go to the study. It's too late to go running. I feel as though the transparent plastic film that protects mobile phones has been ripped off. I'm vulnerable to blows. I shine more. I don't put on a pad.

My neighbour is already writing. I have some binoculars on my desk I use to look at birds, leaves on trees or clouds so I can copy them. He's within touching distance. I can read his screen: 'The house was at the end of the street'.

He sends me a WhatsApp:

'Hello neighbour!' He told me one day that he slept very little. Two or three hours.

'Hwllo!' I write. I add happy, messy emojis. A glass of wine, a pudding, an avocado.

One of the smiling yellow ones from him.

'Whst are you doing swske?' I write.

'Indigestion,' he writes.

'Mt fsult,' I write.

'It was great,' he writes.

I stick my head out the window. I wave. He comes out onto the tiny balcony.

'Everyone's asleep,' I say. 'I was doing some corporate espionage.'

Always these clichés.

'Any leftover champagne?' he asks.

'Yes!' I exclaim happily (too happily). And like a little girl (like an old woman being a little girl) I cover my mouth, suddenly thinking I'll wake everyone up. 'Oops!' And then more quietly. 'Want some?'

'Yes!' he says.

There's an honesty between us two that wasn't there before the party. I am lit up. Soon I'll be ruined. I think about the headlamp I have for running at night. The brightness can be regulated. A round wide beam, or a narrow one. If you tighten it all the way it becomes a square. It lasts while it lasts.

I go down to the kitchen and grab the half-full bottle of champagne from the fridge. My love is still sleeping on the grass, completely abandoned, unkempt. On his back there are red marks from the grass, like the lashes of a whip. I fill two glasses. I go back upstairs. I give him one.

'We'll work better this way,' he says.

'Yes!' I say as happily as before. 'Are you hungry?'

'Yes!'

I go back down and gather canapés, foie-gras, slices of bread and half-finished cheese. I put it all on a plate. I grab my half-full glass and bring it too. I do all this as if it's the last time. I'm using up all my social standing, the consideration he has for me, because I know it'll be completely lost. I jump from my window to his balcony. If I didn't know my future I wouldn't be doing it.

'Champ, eh?' he says to me. He's referring to the Sant Jordi bestsellers.

'I don't care,' I say.

'Okay, okay, you don't care, but amazing, champ!'

'They make the lists then complain that there are lists.'

Each of us says exactly what needs to be said.

'You're the one who makes lists!'

I jump back to my house. He helps me. He squeezes my hand. I grab his finger as if it was a penis through a glory hole. It's the first time in this fifteen-year marriage I've done something so explicit with another man. I know he's thinking the same. I'm doing, committing, a physical euphemism. I'm touching his finger so he can imagine how I would touch his penis. I'm mistreating his wife because Cristina is accidentally mistreating me. I hide. Time to do this shameful act.

In the kitchen I find an ant beside the coffee machine. It's exploring. If I kill it, I'll stop it informing its companions. But others will come. It's only a matter of time.

He awakens, she awakens (she's slept in her room), the little one and her friends awaken (and say they haven't slept at all, but it's not true). All dishevelled, not hungry, like little robots I set going. The garden is full of ashtrays and plastic plates on the tables. The girls say they're not hungry, they don't want milk, if I give them milk they'll vomit. 'We'll puke,' they say.

I try to work out whether he and she remember what happened.

He makes a coffee (Cristina and I look at each other shyly, with a small spark of complicity) and stretches out on the sofa. She says she's going to rehearse on the violin, but doesn't move. He's right, my brother. I made consciously obscene, heightened drawings, where I drew myself deliberately small crying black tears and my uncle and his cock deliberately gigantic, so I'd never be removed from the unit, so it would never occur to them to take me back to the farm. Those drawings were my first works. They were speaking about me, but they were art.

By lunchtime the balance of power has shifted. He and she seem afraid of me. Maybe it's just respect for the elderly. They've done what they wanted to, but they did it by my design. He's certainly fine (it doesn't bother him). She's certainly not. Even though it seems untrue, a young person wants exclusivity, egocentrism in sex. An old person can be promiscuous, doesn't need to be in love, already has been, doesn't even remember it. Yesterday, we didn't think about whether she would get pregnant. It doesn't matter. So be it. We'll sort it out among ourselves. Better that way, that way they won't want to rob the little one from me.

Still as slow as one of the fish he governs from the effect of the drugs, he suggests grilling meat. I understand: it's more social, less intimate. I immediately go to light the fire outside. I know how. They don't. He says: 'We have sausage and chicken in the freezer.' When had he bought and frozen them? The girls' parents come to get them. 'Want champagne?' 'No, no, we're going.'

While running I think:

One night we were watching a National Geographic documentary about the Mayans. They were showing the sculpture of a prisoner who'd been scalped and mutilated. They showed the mouth, wide with pain. There was a bundle of wood on their back, like an explosive belt, because they were to be burned. I was fascinated by this practicality in torture. The well-tied branches had been packed around them so they'd burn well. This conclusion had been reached after tests, trial and error, with many prisoners that maybe didn't end up perfectly singed.

After lunch, the little one has revision to do. He says he's tired, he's falling asleep, partying isn't like before, it'll take days to recover. This hasn't happened to me yet, I'm just sad. Of course, it hasn't happened to Cristina either.

'Wait until nightfall to sleep, otherwise you'll wake up in the middle of the night,' I tell him.

'Yes, yes,' says Cristina.

'What time is it now?' he asks.

'Two minutes past four,' I say. And unconsciously I wipe the face of my running watch.

'Wow, I don't think I'll last. I'm going to bed,' he says.

Then he smiles at us and makes those eyes of a master maker of pâté:

'You two want to come?'

We look at each other. The moment has come.

'No,' I say with a first wife smile. 'Not today. You go, Cristina.'

And she gets up and obeys.

EMPAR MOLINER (SANTA EULÀLIA DE RONÇANA, BARCELONA, 1966) is a Catalan writer and journalist. Her work has been translated into Spanish, German, English and Polish. In 2015 she won the Mercè Rodoreda Prize for *Tot això ho faig perquè tinc molta por*. More recently, in 2022, she won the Ramon Llull Prize for the novel *Benvolguda*, translated into English as Beloved.

LAURA MCGLOUGHLIN HAS BEEN A FREELANCE TRANSLATOR from Catalan and Spanish since completing a Masters in literary translation at the University of East Anglia, and was awarded the inaugural British Centre for Literary Translation Catalan-English Mentorship in 2011. She has translated work by Llüisa Cunillé, Maria Barbal, Flavia Company, Toni Hill Gumbao, Joan Brossa and Bel Olid, and her work has appeared in *The Review of Contemporary Fiction, Asymptote and Metamorphoses*. She was Translator in Residence at the British Centre for Literary Translation during spring 2022. Her most recent translation is The Carnivorous Plant by Andrea Mayo, and forthcoming work includes *The Pocket Guide to Feminism* and *Wanna Fuck*? both by Bel Olid, and Anna Pazos' *Killing the Nerve*.

FROM THE VERY BEGINNING, CATALAN ARTIST AND ARCHITECT Anna Pont worked hand in hand with us. I still remember waking up in the middle of the night with a clear vision: Anna had to be the artist to illustrate our book covers. Her art had exactly the punch that I was looking for. How fortunate I was that Anna accepted the challenge. Her work, always in black and white, was a provocative, rebellious visual act in itself. Anna became part of our identity from day one. She was our Rebel.

Sadly, she died of cancer in the early hours of 18 July 2024 at the age of 48.

In her memory, all proceeds from the sale of this book you are holding in your hands will be donated to fund cancer research.

Anna, you will never be forgotten.

All the love,
Bibiana Mas

Anna Pont (24 July 1975 - 18 July 2024)

We translate female authors who write in minority languages. Only women. Only minority languages. This is our choice.

We know that we only win if we all win, that's why we are proud to be fair trade publishers. And we are committed to supporting organisations in the UK that help women to live freely and with dignity.

We are 3TimesRebel.